WHAT ABOUT THE LOVE PART?

STORIES

STEPHANIE ROSENFELD

BALLANTINE BOOKS
NEW YORK

A Ballantine Book
Published by The Ballantine Publishing Group

Copyright © 2002 by Stephanie Rosenfeld

These stories have appeared, sometimes in different form,
in the following publications:

"Grasp Special Comb," *The Missouri Review,* Spring 1999.
"Good for the Frog," *Cream City Review,* Spring 1995; *Cream City Review
10th Anniversary Anthology,* 1995–1996.
"The Last Known Thing," *Other Voices,* Fall 1994.
"Exactly the Size of Life," *Writers' Forum,* 1993.
"Insects in Amber," *The Best of Writers at Work,* 1993.
"Inversion," *Northwest Review,* Spring 2000.
"How I Went (Recipe for Lime Curd),"
The Bellingham Review, Summer 2000.

www.ballantinebooks.com

Library of Congress Cataloging-in-Publication Data
Rosenfeld, Stephanie, 1968–
What about the love part? : stories / Stephanie Rosenfeld.— 1st ed.
p. ; cm.
ISBN 0-345-44823-5 (alk. paper)
1. United States—Social life and customs—20th century—Fiction. I. Title.
PS3618.O835 W48 2002
813'.6—dc21   2002019746

Text design by Holly Johnson

Manufactured in the United States of America

First Edition: June 2002

10 9 8 7 6 5 4 3 2 1

CONTENTS

ACKNOWLEDGMENTS

Many thanks to Rick Millington and Luciano Colonna for support, financial, domestic, and moral, over the years. Thanks, also, to fellow writers, friends, and generous readers Lida Lewis, Margot Kadesch, and Ann Cannon.

I couldn't have a better agent than Wendy Sherman, or a smarter, more patient editor than Nancy Miller. Thank you for helping me realize this book.

GOOD FOR THE FROG

"I have to tell you," Jasper said to me on the phone—Jasper's the one I tell my boy troubles to. It's a form of flirting, but I keep it carefully reined in, just to the point where he could see it if he were ever to look, but otherwise not. I won't mention how long I've been doing this.

"Jasper's my dream guy," I tell my sort-of boyfriend, Rob, when a glitch in Rob's call-waiting reveals him to be talking to a woman named Emily, whom, he ends up telling me, he thinks he might like to have a life with, though he's never actually gotten up the nerve to ask her on a date.

There's been a string of Robs. I have to remember not

1

to go out with anyone named that anymore, I found myself thinking. Actually, I dreamed that solution, but it seems as much worth trying as anything.

I try to think of what I'll answer if Rob asks me why I said the thing about Jasper—I try to remember what I know about Jasper. He plays an inspired infield; he takes mysterious-looking photographs of houses; he looks right at you when you talk, with intense dark eyes, either brown or blue or green, I can't remember.

He lives three thousand miles away, in San Francisco. Which is the way I like it, I always add to myself heartily, as if I'm telling a joke, working hard to entertain a lone party guest. Also, Jasper netted me a lot of points in the contest my best friend, Sarah, and I devised over the summer, when I was living at her house in Salt Lake City, to round out the long evenings of staying up late talking about her bad dates and listening to the messages left on her answering machine by men she didn't want to talk to. We'd play them over and over, memorizing them, saying them in unison, screaming with laughter.

I worry that it's immature to have this kind of a best friend at thirty-two.

"Are you sure you're not a lesbian?" Rob asked me when I first met him. I was just back from Sarah's, and it must have seemed strange to him that I talked about her so much.

"Listen," I told him, "I wish. Believe me." I stopped just before I told him not to take that personally, that it had nothing to do with the fact that he was phenomenally lousy in bed, and that what was usually going through my head when we'd make love was something like, Shit, I could've gone to the gym. What I'd really like—I didn't tell him this, either—is to ask Sarah to be in my family.

Sarah's and my contest was to see which one of us could become interested in or involved with the most inappropriate man, and Jasper was worth a lot—more, unbelievably, than the celibate fundamentalist born-again Christian I'd tried to convince myself I could change for; more, even— we had to check and recheck this—than the man Sarah was currently seeing, who was fifteen years older than she was, a Republican, married, and living with his wife and four children, two states away. But three thousand miles was worth a lot of points; so was "Probably Has a Girl-friend," and "Isn't Interested in Me." We haven't tallied Rob yet. Sarah hasn't met him, but when she heard me describe him, she said maybe we'd have to invent some new categories.

"I have to tell you," Jasper said. "This might sound harsh, but I think you have kind of a bad attitude toward men." I calculated that he had probably just gotten my letter, in which I'd described a Swing Dance class I'd gone to the night before, and then segued to Rob, and then to Sarah, whom Jasper had never met. "I know this will sound weird,"

I'd said in the letter, "but this summer it was like Sarah became my alter ego, the idea I carried around, and could comfort myself with, by imagining the two of us combined against the evil forces."

I had been, I'd seen at once, the cutest one at the dance class. Not by my own standards, I tried to explain to Jasper. But you know what I'm talking about: the youngest. The fittest. The least plain. The most trophy-like, perhaps? The class was made up mostly of single men and women. The women, like the men, were in their late thirties and early forties, generally unhip but pleasant looking. No one was talking to them.

First, a very short bald man about seventeen years older than me came over to where I was leaning against the wall waiting for class to start, introduced himself, and told me I was an attractive woman. He gave me a rundown of every dance event happening in the region and asked a lot of questions I was afraid to answer, because of the way they seemed to be pointing toward an invitation. Finally, just as I was considering drawing myself up to my full height to see if that would make the man go away, he nodded and moved on, and into his place stepped a red-faced guy, a little closer to my age, with a fresh stain on his shirt, who stuck out his hand and told me his name, and asked me if I had registered as a leader or a follower, and if I was a follower, would I be his partner when the dancing started?

I told Jasper that I'd begun to feel a little bit like a fire hydrant at a dog convention; I told him about the guy who rubbed his hand down my back when I rotated to his position during the lesson and said, "Are you feeling comfortable with this?" in a voice that made me glance around to see if anyone else had heard; and about the one who kept looking anxiously at the guy before him in the rotation, and who finally said, "God, he must be really good. All the women are, like, *panting* by the time they get to me. Is he? Really good?"

"Don't take this the wrong way," I'd written. "But I left there feeling like . . . I'm sorry, but feeling like there's something really wrong with men.

"I mean," I'd continued lamely. "I'm not saying there is. But *is* there?"

"This will sound even weirder," I'd written, and I told him about one weekend in the summer, when Sarah was out of town—how I went on a date with a man who actually said, "I'm a hunter, and you're the hunted—I saw what I wanted and I went out and got it"; and how the next day I met a man in a coffee shop who told me he knew in his heart he was an artist, because he had always wanted to make a sculpture by wrapping a woman in cheesecloth and

spraying her with a lot of spray starch; and how, shortly after he left, another man came over to my table and said,
"You've got nice long legs," and asked if I'd like to go out
with him, and when I told him he might find me pretty
hostile, had said, "Hey!" and thrown his hands in the air,
"It's not like I want to *marry* you or anything."

"This is the weird part, I guess," I wrote to Jasper, but
then I sat there staring—not writing, just remembering:
When I got home, I was shaking. I'd walked from one
room of Sarah's apartment to the next, breathing hard, my
throat tight.

I didn't know where the dry, panicky feeling was coming from, but after a minute I realized what it reminded me
of: I was remembering being five years old, one evening
when my mother left me alone in the house with my sleeping baby brother while she went to pick up my father at the
train station.

The radio had been on, to a classical station, when all
of a sudden the music went away and loud, terrifying static
filled the room. I didn't know what to do—I started running around in circles, my hands in the air. I remember
looking down as I ran, at the wide bands of our red-and-
blue braided rug, curving like a racetrack beneath my feet.
Finally I'd run from the house and up the road and gotten
the neighbor woman, who hadn't understood a word I was
trying to say, and who, when she came into the house and
heard the radio, and saw me pointing mutely at it, had said,
"You stupid little girl; why didn't you just turn it off?"

———

Finally, that day at Sarah's, I calmed down a little. My circuit through the rooms slowed, and I went to the kitchen and opened the dish cupboard. I didn't want anything, exactly—somehow, just standing there looking at Sarah's dishes was making me feel better.

When I have a life I like better, in a place I want to stay, I want to live like Sarah. Sarah's apartment is full of small, beautiful objects made by artisans in the places she travels to for her work as a museum consultant—luminous ceramic bowls; handmade books with leather closures, bone clasps, and flecked, pulpy pages; framed woodcuts; brightly painted clay animal sculptures.

My favorite of all these things sits on top of her microwave—a tiny, hand-pinched cup and saucer. The cup, about the size of a crab apple, is the hollow head of a man, painted brightly and whimsically with black swirls of hair, a swirling mustache, dancing cerulean eyes, rosy circles for cheeks. His ears, jutting from the side of his face, form tiny handles. It's not just that I like the cup—I also like to picture Sarah finding it and buying it. It would never occur to me, I realized—even if I saw it in a gallery, and had the money in my pocket—that I could own such a thing, that it was something I could buy for myself and bring home to live with me.

———

Finally I took a big, handblown cranberry-red glass tumbler from the cupboard. It was the one I always chose—I liked the feel of it in my hands. The glass was thin and fragile, with a bumpy texture like big blisters, and it was almost too big to hold in one hand. I liked the way I felt like a little kid when I drank from it, three-quarters of my face disappearing into its cool, dark mouth.

I filled the glass with ice and water and took it to my room. I set it down on my desk and I stripped off the clothes I had worn to the café, letting them fall in a pile on the floor. Next to them, in another pile, were the clothes I had worn the night before on my date with the hunter. He had been wearing some kind of vile cologne, and I could still smell it.

The hunter had taken me to his "place," which had turned out to be not an apartment, but a bar that he owned. Due to a lack of the proper licenses, it wasn't yet open to the public.

He had produced wine and fruit from the refrigerator behind the bar, and a loaf of bread, and we had been having a not unpleasant conversation, about what, I can't remember. He hadn't yet likened me to quarry, and I hadn't yet gotten the sudden and strong sensation that I wasn't the first woman to play a part in this particular scenario.

After a short time, he'd gotten up abruptly and gone over to a panel on the wall and started fiddling with knobs. The lights went down around me and came up a low, glowing purple on the other side of the room over a small parquet dance floor.

"Do you want to dance?" the hunter asked.

I did and I didn't. The music was loud, lilting reggae. It had been a long time since I'd moved my body to a rhythm from outside myself—not private and still and contained, and entirely hidden from anyone else's view. It had been almost a year since Stephen left me, and I'd barely talked to a man in that time.

I wanted to stand under the purple lights. I wanted to turn my back and close my eyes and sway. But I didn't want to have to look at this man or talk to him; I didn't want to have to think about what I was doing, or try to calculate the limits of his control or lack of it; I didn't want to cause a misunderstanding; I didn't want to be raped.

There was a half-finished letter to Jasper on my computer screen. I stood in my underwear for a minute, looking at the letter. It was the one I worked on and never sent. It had started out wrong, somehow, and I couldn't get it right. I would labor over the words and sentences, but each thing I wrote seemed to make the thing that came before it, or the thing that came after it, wrong.

So how are things in California, was the last line I'd written; I saw now that I had already used the tired segue in another place. I deleted the line and wrote, Here's what happened to me today. Then I deleted "today" and wrote "yesterday."

I went out with a man I didn't particularly like. It's been a year since Stephen left. I can't remember what's a good reason to do anything or not do it. I danced with him. I let him put his hands on me. I didn't like it, and I didn't not like it—it just felt like hands on skin. I touched him, too. I looked at my hands and not at him; I watched them move and thought about odd things—trucks on roads, barges on rivers, ponderous vehicles on their way to the next place.

He kissed me and I kissed him back; I kissed him a long time, not because I liked him, but because I was trying to identify some feeling, any feeling. It was nothing—nothingness trying to bubble its way in through my lips. I tried not to think about Stephen.

I let him take off my clothes, and I stood there in the purple light while he looked at me. He was still dancing. "You are a beautiful woman," he said, and I finally felt something—some terrible, painful thing swelling inside, as if the nothingness had gone in through my mouth and was filling me, like a poisonous, bubbling liquid.

"I'd like to be inside you," he said, and at first I didn't understand what he meant. I was picturing my insides, the way they felt since Stephen left—bare and sterile and angular as an empty white room. Then I'd looked down, and I saw what he meant, and I was glad, at least, that I'd found some line not to cross.

But, God, Jasper, I'd written. Why am I telling you this? and then I'd deleted all of it and written, So how are things in California? Salt Lake City is okay; the men are kind of weird.

Standing there in front of the computer in my underwear, I'd looked down at my body. "You are a beautiful woman," I said, like someone trying out words in a foreign language. I thought about the way the words, each time they've been said to me, have become linked with something bad, in my memory—some pain or disappointment, or humiliation, or betrayal.

I thought about how I like my body, when I'm alone with it. I stretched a leg out to the side and flexed. My legs are strong.

I biked twelve miles straight uphill yesterday, I wrote in Jasper's letter. "Your legs are strong," the hunter had said to me. "I'd like to be between those legs."

Whenever men said that to me, I would have a memory, which was usually inappropriate to the moment, of something that happened when I was four or five years old: I had found a frog, and made a box for it to live in on the sunporch, with some grass and branches and rocks and a dish of water. The first day, though, I couldn't leave it alone; I kept going in and catching it, picking it up, wanting to feel once more the texture of its cold, bumpy skin against my hand.

"Look," I'd said to my mother, and I'd showed her the way when I squeezed the frog's belly, its throat would swell like a big, white bubble, and its mouth would open slightly, as if it wanted to say something.

"I don't know if that's good for the frog, honey," my mother had said. She was right. The next morning, when I went out to greet it, the frog was dead. I'd put it in the bushes without telling anybody, but I still feel a twinge of shame whenever I think about it.

When Jasper said the thing about my bad attitude, I took a deep breath. I felt my stomach turn familiarly—the reflexive and indiscriminate sensation of having done something wrong.

"No, let me explain," I wanted to say, but I didn't, because I didn't know what I would say after that.

"So what about this guy you're seeing?" Jasper said, after a minute.

"Rob," I answered. Rob is the kind of boyfriend who inspires comments like, "So what is it you said you liked about this man, again?" from my friends.

"Would it be offensive of me to suggest that that's a Major Red Flag?" Sarah had asked me the last time we talked on the phone. I'd been describing something Rob had done or said.

"But basically he's a good person," I'd said. "Maybe I just have to get used to him. I think he has the *potential* to be a good guy."

"Is it time for me to do the thing you asked me to?" said Sarah.

I'd written her a letter shortly after I started going out with Rob. Here it is in writing, I'd said, and I want you to keep this letter and read it back to me in two months when I come running to you with a broken heart: This man is not for me. He's selfish, uncommunicative, sexually dysfunctional, dishonest, and he's not even nice to me.

I can *see* all that from here, I'd written. So why can't I just trust my own authority and get rid of him now?

Because you can't, Sarah had written back comfortingly. Because you're programmed to do something else.

"Don't I have a will, though?" I'd asked her on the phone. "To make a decision and act on it?"

"It's like thinking about the cake on top of the refrigerator," said Sarah. "Making the decision with your brain that you're not going to have any frees you to go over and start picking."

"Nothing ever looks black and white," I'd said.

"Nothing ever *is* black and white," Sarah answered. "That's our power. The ability to turn everything gray."

"Oh, Rob," I said to Jasper on the phone. "It's not working out that well. He's a little screwed up."

"I want him to be a good guy," I'd said to Sarah the last time we talked, hearing the way it sounded like a question.

"Ah," Sarah had said. "I think we've identified the problem. Do you hear yourself? You *want*."

"Don't get me wrong," I added, to Jasper. "It's not my attitude. I realize he doesn't represent all men."

"Unless," I'd said to Sarah, "he embodies the concept, distilled to its purest form."

"He doesn't like intimacy," I said to Jasper.

"Oh yeah?" said Jasper. Curiously or cautiously, I couldn't tell.

"Uh-oh," Sarah had said, when I told this to her. Then, "How can you tell?"

"He came right out and said it. . . ." My voice trailed off. "That's good, right? That at least he knows it?"

"Um," said Sarah. "Who am I supposed to be in this conversation? Your loyal friend who supports you in everything you do, or would you like a reality check?"

"Rob says he thinks love is basically just a mental construct, and we could probably all do fine without it."

"Well, why does he want to be in relationships with women, then?" Sarah had asked.

"I don't know. I listen to his problems a lot," I said. "He talks about his ex-girlfriend a lot. He talks about the girlfriend he hopes to have, sometime in the future."

"Huh?" said Sarah.

"The perfect woman for him. He doesn't know who

she is, but he knows I'm not her. He says maybe that's why he can't be truly intimate with me."

"Wait a minute," said Sarah. "So he *does* want intimacy?"

"Well, he says he wants to be free right now," I told her.

"Free to what?"

" 'To have sex,' is what he said."

"Wait. Aren't you having sex?" Sarah said.

"He means, to have sex with a lot of people. He says everyone wants that. Actually, what he said was, right now he thought he just wanted to be able to fuck anything that moved."

"Neat," Sarah said.

"I can't believe he meant it," I said. "It's hard to picture, for one thing. It would have to be something that moved pretty slow."

This is what I wanted to tell Jasper, I know now, in the letter I hadn't sent this summer: that that afternoon at Sarah's had felt like the center of something, a moment after which things wouldn't be the same.

Things won't even be the same between you and me, I wanted to say, but that didn't make sense, since there had never been any Jasper and me.

That day, I'd turned off the computer and then realized I hadn't saved Jasper's file. I tried to calculate how much would be lost, though it didn't matter at all.

Finally I'd slipped on some clothes—a loose tank top that Sarah had given me, no bra underneath, and a pair of cool, loose jersey shorts, also Sarah's. Sarah's a little bigger than I am, and I liked the feel of the outfit—the way the cotton enfolded me and swished around me when I walked.

Putting on the clothes made me start to feel better. I was already reconstituting the story of my date in my head, thinking of the way I would tell it to Sarah, looking for the little things that would make her laugh. I was glad I hadn't bothered her at her hotel in Toronto the night before. She had left the number, in case of emergency, and I had lain on her bed next to the phone for a long time after I came in, looking at the slip of paper, calculating and recalculating the time difference, thinking about the word "emergency."

After I got dressed, I left the house and got in my car and I drove, from one end of the city to the other—first to a pawn shop I had seen on the West side, then to an artisans' collective on the East bench, then to another place, a used-clothing boutique at the bottom of the Hill, not far from Sarah's.

It was something I'd been meaning to do all summer and hadn't. I'd been saving my money; this shopping spree was going to be my one indulgence, when I'd figure out why I deserved it.

In the pawn shop, I bought a silver ring, plain, slightly flawed. I put it on the fourth finger of my right hand and stretched my arm away. I never wore jewelry. I admired the way the ring made my hand look like somebody else's.

At the artisans' collective I decided on a thick, filigreed silver band from Bali for the middle finger of my right hand, and for the middle finger of my left, a narrow twist of silver. There was a twisted silver bracelet at the place near Sarah's, and I bought that, too.

I wanted to tell Jasper how I'd felt, glancing down at my wrist and hands in the car, feeling the unfamiliar light pressure around my fingers, the just-discernible glancing of metal against my skin. I'd felt resourceful. Protected. And, I'd been thinking, pleased with the neatness of this solution, if only I remembered to put the jewelry on every time I went out of the house, I could keep this feeling.

I didn't tell Jasper, though. Even Sarah hadn't seemed to understand exactly, though she'd listened and nodded her head when I told her. When I picked her up at the airport, she'd looked at my wrist and hands and said, in a tone that puzzled me, "Oh, look at all your silver."

I'd made it into a joke—related the events of the weekend, told her about feeling besieged by the evil forces; about driving around, deranged, and buying the jewelry. She'd laughed, and made sympathetic comments; then, when we were home, she'd given me a bemused look, and handed me a small box with a thin silver bracelet inside.

"I don't know about the evil forces," she said, "but when I saw this, I thought of you."

"Anyway," I said into the telephone, to Jasper. "None of it's that important. It's all for the best. He's not what I want."

I couldn't believe I'd let those words slip out. I imagined all the red lights and sirens going off in Jasper's head.

"Hmm," he said, his voice unreadable. "What *do* you want?"

"Oh," I answered. "I don't know. Something easy. Something fun. Maybe I just want to be able to—what do you say?—fuck anything that moves."

"Whoa," Jasper said, sounding interested. "Really?"

"No," I answered. "Not really. Did it sound good?"

"I don't know," he said, after a minute.

"So," he said. "It sounds like you've had some bad dates lately. Salt Lake City. It sounds like maybe you better stay away from that place."

"Yeah," I said.

"Don't come here, though," he said. "San Francisco—not fun for single straight women, from what I hear. Me, on the other hand. I'm like a kid in a candy store."

Red Flag, comes a weakened little voice from somewhere. I'm getting my images mixed up: I see someone drowning, calmly, like in the cartoons—going down for the last time. She waves her red flag weakly, but when I look again, it's gone, dropped into the ocean. Now she raises her almost-limp hand, the index finger bent feebly in the air, like someone who wanted to make a point. Then I see her again—first the finger and hand, then the woman attached to it—on a street in some big city, still alive, somehow, but still growing feebler, hailing a cab that won't come.

"So what do *you* want?" I was just about to ask Jasper. Later, I was glad I didn't get to ask the question—he spoke first.

"Hey, what about this Sarah?" he said, and I remembered I'd told him in the letter that my best friend was moving to San Francisco.

She's tall and beautiful, blazingly intelligent, self-confident, funny, interesting, and cool, I'd said, and I remembered feeling an odd sense of loss as I wrote it. I was imagining myself being made up of particles that I could see breaking up around my edges: small parts of me—parts I didn't need in and of themselves, but still—dancing away into brightness.

"Ah," I said, stalling for time so that my voice wouldn't sound funny. "You want to meet Sarah."

Jasper laughed, too quickly, too much. "You make her sound so tempting," he said.

"I do," I said, stupidly. "She is. She's great."

After I came back to the house, the day I bought the rings and the bracelet, I'd gone into my bedroom to take off my shoes. I'd forgotten about the red glass; it sat sweating on the desk. I picked it up and went into the kitchen to refill it, then I brought it into the living room and set it down again.

Outside, it had been almost too hot to breathe, but the living room was cool and dark. I turned on the stereo and lay down on my back on Sarah's Oriental rug. The rug had a dark, complicated design right in the middle of it; sometimes, when I'd stand at one edge of the room, it looked like an opening to me, a dark gash that the rest of the rug's colors and patterns might slide off into. I lay in the middle of the rug. It wasn't very big, and like a kid, I pulled in my hands and feet, every strand of my hair, so that none of me touched the floor.

I put my feet up on a chair at the edge of the rug and I looked at my brown thighs. I imagined squeezing the life out of something. Then I imagined pumping up a canyon on my bicycle—the satisfaction of not stopping for anything, of riding through the pain.

I imagined running, like in the dreams I sometimes had—not chasing and not being pursued, but just going, getting faster and stronger and less and less tired the farther I went.

I thought about the hunter. After he'd told me he wanted to be inside me, he'd cleared one of the restaurant

tables and told me to get on it. He'd seemed genuinely surprised when I started putting on my clothes.

I got up and went over and turned up the music. It was
just what Sarah had left in the CD player—some jazz, not
dancing music at all—but I stood in the middle of the red
rug and started to sway with my eyes closed, my head
tipped back, slowly at first, and then faster. I raised my arms
and snaked them around in the air; I twirled, with my eyes
still shut. I danced faster and faster, and when I got dizzy, I
opened my eyes and looked down, and I danced like that:
my sight filled with the rug's familiar pattern and colors
and texture, until I was flushed and sweating, and the image
of the night before, the purple lights and the parquet and
the memory of the hunter's hands on my body, had lifted
and dissolved like an unclean fog burning off the landscape.

"Yeah," I said to Jasper, "you'll like Sarah," and I tried to
picture Sarah and Jasper on a date.

The way I was picturing it, though, I was there, too,
the three of us around a round table. They were both smiling slightly, looking in my direction. I pushed my chair
back a little, so that they were closer to each other than
they were to me.

I smiled, and raised my glass of dark, cold beer to my
lips. Sarah had lent me a fringed red Indian-print silk scarf
to wear, and I had draped it around my neck. I liked the

way my thick, dark hair tangled over it. I looked beautiful, I knew. I'd just made Sarah laugh; she was rocked back in her chair, balancing there for a second. She tossed her red curls. I tossed my brown ones. It's something we do involuntarily—contagious hair-flipping, from being girls together. It annoys other women. Men like it. Jasper looked from her to me.

"You guys are awesome," he said, but then I realized it wasn't his voice I was imagining. It was something someone else—one of Sarah's dates in the summer—had said. That time, I'd really tagged along. Sarah had invited me to help keep the evening light; the guy had been coming on too strong, she said.

We'd looked at each other with our can-we-remember-this-for-later? looks, because we both knew that what the man meant was not awesome, but scary. We'd been talking and laughing nonstop, getting more and more cynical, and the subject had turned to men. The last guy Sarah had gone out with had told her she made him uncomfortable because he suspected she might be smarter than he was. He'd met a cruel fate on Sarah's answering machine. We were still quoting him.

"We're not *all* bad," this new date had said, working carefully to match our jollity. I'd looked at Sarah and flared my nostrils.

"No," she said politely. "You're not. As individuals, many of you are very nice." She flared back.

"Yeah," I said. I'd be the troublemaker, just in case she

wanted to go out with this guy again. "Some of you have your good point." We ran our hands through our hair.

I was trying to imagine the conversation Sarah and I would have after our date with Jasper. I pictured us walking into her new place and turning on the lights, taking off our shoes, turning on the TV, getting into T-shirts. I went into the kitchen. "Do you know what you want?" I called.

"What?" she called back, as if she hadn't understood.

"Do you *want* anything?"

"Yeah," she answered.

"What?"

"Whatever you've got," she yelled.

I got a bottle of water out of the refrigerator and went to the cupboard. I saw that she hadn't even unpacked everything yet. I took out the red glass.

When I got back to the other room, Sarah was sprawled on the couch, looking at a magazine. She threw it down when I came in. I set the glass on the coffee table that I'd given her as a housewarming present. She'd never had a coffee table; we were always noticing the lack, in her old place.

"You can't give me this," she'd said. My father had made it just before he died; it was solid oak, plain, quite handsome.

"Just for now," I told her, though I knew I'd never take it back. "Just till I have a place I want to put it."

"That was stupid," I said as I set the glass down, "I only brought one." I sat down, anyway, on the floor across from Sarah. "You can have it," I told her.

"We can share it," she said, but neither of us reached for the glass. I put my arms on the coffee table and leaned my chin on my fist. Through the glass, I could see the dark, blurry shape of Sarah. It looked like another place, where she was.

I shifted my focus so that I was looking at the glass's surface; I had a sudden image of my body sliding down vast, icy walls, the big blistery protrusions banging against my ribs, hollowing out my stomach, like something that ought to hurt, but didn't.

On the other side of the glass, Sarah ran her hand through her hair lazily. She let her arm stay raised in the air for a minute, and it seemed to take her hair a long time to fall, bit by bit, back to her face.

I sat up. I was looking into the glass now, into the icy life inside its thin red walls, and I thought about the way the glass was deceptively light when it was empty, so that my hand, going to heft it off the shelf, would sometimes almost launch it into the empty air of the kitchen.

I thought about the hunter, telling me he wanted to be inside of me; and about Rob, and Stephen—all of them; about the way they all said that, eventually; and I had another picture—of all of them, inside of me, wandering around as if they might find something in there, as if I were a hall, or the bright, white room I kept dreaming Stephen in after he left.

"So what'd you think of Jasper?" I asked Sarah. I took a drink and held out the glass to her. She raised herself up and took it from me, but she didn't drink. She lay back down, balancing the glass on her chest.

It seemed important to me, suddenly, to know where the glass had come from; it seemed strange that I didn't. But I didn't want to ask Sarah, because of the way I know she is: When she finds out I like something of hers, she usually finds a way to give it to me.

I was listening for Sarah's answer—I was listening for the sound of her voice. But if she said anything, I didn't hear it, because all of a sudden I got distracted thinking about how I was going to lose all my points that I'd racked up with Jasper, and she was going to get them, and others besides, probably.

I was wondering what I was going to do, to not be left in the dust. I was wishing, for some reason, that Sarah would take a drink. I'd forgotten to breathe, I realized, as I watched the icy red glass rising and falling on Sarah's chest.

I sat up and reached for the glass just at the moment Sarah raised it to her lips.

"Go for it," I said, but she held it out to me, and for a second it was as if neither one of us were touching it—the way it hung there magically in the air between us, weightless as a wish, a small planet held aloft by the amazing gravity-suspending powers of our fingertips.

GRASP SPECIAL COMB

PEDICULOSIS: IDENTIFICATION AND TREATMENT

by

Abigail Randall-Hillman

Pediculus humanis capitus, the common—

- Return library books
- UC Science lib: Pediculosis, *pediculicides,* pyrethrin, permethrin
- Call Mom

PEDICULOSIS AND YOUR CHILD
by
Abigail L. Randall

- Buy bagels
- Check to V. Sch. of Ballet

PEDICULUS HUMANIS CAPITUS:
ONE WILY MOTHERF——— (ha)

- Katrin: New leotard
  Ponytail holders
- Call Mom

YOUR CHILD AND HEAD LICE
by
Abby Hillman (Katrin Hillman, Group 2B)

Head lice is a common childhood _____ that can be
present in any segment of the population at any given time.

- Disease, illness, malady, condition. Affliction.
- Afflict: to humble, overthrow, try, torment, torture,
  rack
- Personal nuisance problem (Hamp. Cty DPH)

- Rack (!)—Racked with lice

If your child comes home from school with head lice, don't be alarmed.

- Pharmacy: Nix (big size)
    Egg-dissolver stuff
    Metal comb (check w/ Gary—did he
      take mine?)
    More of those plastic clampy things
- Cash

If your child comes home from school with head lice, try not to be alarmed.

- Do laundry (check w/ Ed re: Why no hot H_2O?)
- Borrow vacuum (check w/ Gary—Why does he get vacuum; split cost of new one?)
- Katrin: Cancel play date w/ Chiara
      "   "   "   "/ Ariana
    Practice
    Wash and comb
- Comb Leon?
- Call Leon: Does he have magnifying glass at work?

If your child comes home with head lice, try not to panic.

- Call Mom
- Grocery store: More laundry det.

Garbage bags (big)

Dinner??

Treat for Katrin

• Video/book-on-tape for K. (unabridged)

If your child comes home with head lice—

THE TRUTH ABOUT HEAD LICE

by

Abby Randall

Head lice is a scourge from hell that will temporarily ruin your life and possibly damage it permanently.

• Kind of strong. Stick to facts.

Head lice, *pediculus humanis capitus*, are tiny black, gray, or brown.

• tiny insects, very difficult to see, which
• insects so small, it's difficult to see them at all, let alone tell what color they are
• tiny, moving, transparent, black-hearted specks and their eggs, malevolent grains of next-to-nothing-ness that attach themselves to the hair shaft at the scalp's surface and have the capacity to rob you of every crumb of hope, peace of mind, optimism, or

spiritual ease you might at one time have possessed, not to mention sanity, sleep, and every free moment from the present to some far-off point in the increasingly unimaginable nit-free future.

There are a number of over-the-counter remedies available, all of which are expensive and none of which work. Their packages are printed with blatant lies, which a perky member of your HMO's Advice Staff ("This is Donna in A. S.") will read to you over the phone, until you realize the words sound familiar. You ask if anyone there's ever actually had lice. You ask if anyone there's ever seen your child's head of hair, when Miss A. S. says people do survive this, all you have to do is comb every strand of your child's hair two times each day, wash all the bedding in hot water every day, vacuum the entire house and the car, every day. "Steam-cleaning works best," she reads, "or you can simply close off the entire area: playroom, TV room—anywhere the kids spend a lot of time—for fourteen days."

When she tells you, as if this is the way stupid people get lice in the first place, not to let children share brushes, clothing, or headgear, and says, "There *is* a prescription available, but we don't like to use it except as a last resort," as if she wants you to beg her for a substance that will give your child permanent nerve damage, you say, "Headgear, Miss Verbatim?"; you tell her you're guessing she doesn't have any children, ask her how many rooms in *her* mansion. You ask what A. S. stands for again, Attitude Spewing?, then you thank her for the "advice," and hang up.

This is day two of lice; this is before you understand that lice can be used to measure many things: the shortness of a day; the ferocity of your instinct to kill things that attack your child; the natural amounts of pessimism and optimism you possess; the number of days remaining in your life.

- What happened to facts?
- Check w/ Gary re: health coverage after divorce
- Call Mom

FACTS
- Lice range from 2mm–4mm in size. Life cycle
  from nit to adult is 16–21 days. Adult lice live
  about 30 days. They will die of starvation if kept off
  their host's body for more than 10 days. Cannot survive temperatures above 128.3°F for more than 5
  minutes.
- Lice need the blood of human beings to survive
  and will die naturally within 24 hours if they cannot
  find human blood.
- Which is it—10 days or 24 hrs.?
- Female head louse glues eggs to the base of hairs.
  Will deposit between 50–150 eggs in her lifetime.
  Eggs hatch in 5–10 days. Human hair grows about
  ½ inch per month. Therefore, any nits found on a

¼ inch from scalp would be approximately 16 days old and probably will not hatch.

• Cancel hair appt.

FACTS
• Anyone can get lice regardless of his/her degree of personal hygiene.
• Caucasian children are most likely to get lice.
• Lice can affect you mentally (Explain).

Lice might make you remember strange, unrelated things. Cooties, cootie spray, being a kid; sitting in the woods in Memory Grove with Maddy Jacobs and Jimmy Colon talking about the ghost you're supposed to be able to see there at night, walking across the road. Either she was a jilted bride or got hit by a car or both. Maddy saying, Let's play Flip Your Top, telling you how: You pull your shirt up, just for a second, so Jimmy can see underneath. You remember being confused about a few things, like the way you felt when she said, "You *have* to." You believed the words were true, and it gave you kind of a sick ache, almost as if your life was over. It's the same thing you'll feel when you get lice, when it's six-thirty and dinner's not even started and you realize you still have to wash all the bedding—all the sheets and pillowcases and the towels, at the laundromat, no less, since Gary got to keep the appliances—before anyone can go to bed tonight. You *have* to. Why didn't Jimmy have to do anything? Why did he get to sit there, his face impassive, and watch you expose your lumpy, embarrassing chest?

- Too personal (?) Get back on track.

Even though the memories it brings up aren't that great, lice might make you wish you were a kid again. The year of the great fruit-and-nut wars—crab apple, plum, horse chestnut fights on the way home from school. Any ripe, rotting, eye-sized projectile you could get your hands on. Always, boys against girls. You might suddenly, intensely miss the manic abandon of that time, that state of grace, the intense, single-minded will to do damage to the enemy, without thought of consequence.

- Cancel Jessica for Saturday night/ Can she baby-sit sometime late Nov.?
- Cancel Katrin dentist
- Call Mom

Or trying on bathing suits at the mall with your friend, Denise, complaining about your moms—you might suddenly remember that.

Combing Katrin's hair in the graying afternoon light, re-membering trying on red bathing suits with Denise, the year of the Farrah Fawcett poster, in adjacent dressing rooms at

Nobby in the Fashion Place Mall, talking to each other over the walls of the stalls—"Judy turned my white cords pink in the wash and she won't even give me money to buy another pair," "I swear to God Barb's going through the change,"—you might get an unexpected pang, something wandering off in a wrong direction; you might suddenly wish for someone to take care of you—even the person whose goal in life, you knew, was to make you think you were insane—your mother.

- What is the prob.?!! Get back to facts.
- Difference betw. head lice & body lice
- Crabs

Or it might make you remember college: It might make you think about your best friend, then, Randi. Denise was long gone by this time, engaged to a Mormon, friends with her mother. Randi took notes in Modern American Literature once on a box of Nilla Wafers she ate on the way to class.

"We're going to be late," you complained, as you stood in line at the Sunshine Farm at eight in the morning, waiting for her to buy the cookies.

"So go," she said. But there was something about Randi—you couldn't leave her, bleary-eyed in her huge sweatshirt and boxer shorts, at the checkout.

"What's white and crawls up your leg?" Randi said. Something on the shelf behind you had caught her eye. "Uncle Ben's Perverted Rice," she answered herself.

That's the kind of thing you might remember, sitting in front of *Pippi in the South Seas*, combing strand by strand: You might start thinking about how romance, marriage, whatever it is you are attempting to do with your boyfriend, that you attempted to do with boys back then, obscures most other kinds of love. And how Randi cracking her joke, not even looking at you but smiling into the corner, your presence required but not acknowledged, was a kind of love, though you didn't know it at the time: offered sideways, received quietly, an underlying condition and not a daily negotiation, and what does that have to do with lice? What does that have to do with you, as you sit in the darkening living room, combing Katrin's hair? She is trying to be good, but tears leak out of the corners of her eyes. The health center literature suggests you "keep squirmy kids in place with a Popsicle"; what kid wouldn't see this as a bogus non sequitur? You start to laugh.

"Why are you laughing, Mom?" Katrin says, crying, then laughing a little, too.

"I had this friend once in college." You have never told Katrin about Randi.

"What was she like?"

You try to remember what, about Randi, would be appropriate to tell a child. Once, drunk and high on coke, the two of you shot a tube of toothpaste in a fraternity bathroom with a bow and arrow. Once, at a party, Randi walked past a boy who had dumped her and said, in a conversational tone just loud enough for everyone to hear, "Dave Cooney? Premature ejaculator."

"Does Randi have kids?" asks Katrin.

"A little girl, Jane, I think."

Katrin thinks about this for a minute, then says, "Maybe Jane has lice, too."

• Product info. instead?

>Nix—permethrin; low toxicity, kills lice and eggs in one ten-minute treatment.

>Rid—pyrethrin-based, not as effective at killing nits.

>Kwell—lindane, prescription only, also not as good at killing nits. (Yet is more toxic. What is deal?)

>Malathion lotion—must stay on head for 8–12 hours.

• Problems re: putting a product called malathion lotion on your child's head for 8–12 hours.

FACTS

• Nix is 95% effective (according to Nix). Its lice-killing effects continue to work for up to fourteen days. May be used again after 7–10 days. (Not necessary, but recommended.) (?)

• Lice can be eliminated from unwashable items by sealing in a plastic bag for a minimum of 14 days.

However, 35 days is better in order to eliminate risk from any dormant egg.

• Dormant egg?

If your child comes home from school with head lice, try not to panic. There are several over-the-counter products, called pediculicides, which claim—

They all claim to kill lice and their eggs, but it's a crock! There is always one left alive. Every mother you talk to will look at you with round eyes, twitching head, and say, "They lie. The packages lie. I put a whole bottle of (X) on (Olivia/Elspeth/Ariel's) head, and the next day a LIVE BUG walked across her scalp."

There are several over-the-counter products, which, combined with careful, (thorough, vigilant, scrupulous, maniacal)—

A special, fine-toothed comb must be used to remove nits. Divide hair into one-inch squares. Grasp special comb at an angle, with smooth side slanted backward—

You can throw around the expressions "nit-picking" and "go through with a fine-toothed comb," but until your child actually comes home with lice, you can't really appreciate the meaning of the words; you will feel foolish, sheepish, for ever having used them lightly, you will feel annoyed, enraged, murderous toward people who commit this offense around you.

"*Have you really?*" you might say to your boss, when he says he's been going over the payroll with a fine-toothed comb and uncovered a little problem in your department.

"*A fine-toothed comb,*" you say. Lice makes you talk in italics; it makes you impatient with the people you loathe. It wipes out the pleasantries, zooms you right to the heart of things. "*Interesting you should put it that way.*"

"*These are baked goods we're talking about, right?*" you might say, when he says he wasn't going to mention it, but now that you've taken everything to such a negative level, yesterday's cookies were too big. "*It's not like I put the baboon heart in the wrong patient, though, is it?*" you might say. You might actually yell that. "It's not like anyone *died, right?* It's not like anyone *got lice.*"

When your boss tells you he's putting you on notice, you jump up from the table. "*You're* putting *me* on notice. That's rich." Lice makes you sound like Fred Flintstone.

You put all the men in your life on notice.

"Oh, when I'm *nit-picking, Leon,* you'll know it," you blurt to your up-till-now-perfectly-good boyfriend, when he chooses the unfortunate phrase to tell you that you remind him of his mother.

"What do *you* know about *nit-picking?*" you imagine yourself challenging the next boyfriend, the one in the unimaginable future. Even men from the past—all the old boyfriends who left for one reason or another—suddenly fall into one of two new categories: those who could have weathered an infestation with you, and the rest.

• (Lice as evolutionary tool in boyfriend selection)

Lice might cause you to dissociate more than usual; you might find yourself thinking about the desert, where you once lived; you can picture the lice dying of dehydration, staggering backward off your head like bad guys in a movie. You can feel your scalp baking in the cleansing heat, hear the trickle of water, like a new beginning, in a dry wash.

You might picture these things while your boyfriend is screaming, "*I* didn't bring lice into this house!" It is the day after the first treatment and combing. He has reached his limit already. You have slipped and said that your one set of clean sheets is *at home*. In your dryer, in your ex-husband's house. Technically still your house, too. "In the dryer," you say. "Gary's dryer. *My* dryer. For God's sake. Whatever." It gets confusing. Technically, also, Gary is not yet your ex. You will get around to getting divorced one day soon. After the refinance goes through and you've gotten rid of lice.

"I don't really like the doing-your-laundry-at-Gary's-thing," he's said, again. He's mentioned it a few times. It makes him uncomfortable to think there's some kind of an unspoken connection lingering between you and Gary and he would prefer it if you lugged your laundry, and Katrin's, to the Laundromat.

You warned this man, when he was pursuing you, "It's not going to be the way you think it's going to be."

"Let's go to Baja," he said. Morocco, Indonesia, the Golden Triangle. Hot, sultry nights; the two of you in a little shack on the beach or in the jungle, lying in a bed canopied by mosquito netting, reading books by candlelight, listening to shortwave radio.

"I've never been in a long-term, monogamous relationship before," he said. "I'd really like to try it with you." He was surprised by your response, angry.

"Is that supposed to sound like a qualification to me?" you asked.

You don't say to him now that if he doesn't like the idea of the doing-your-laundry-at-Gary's-thing, then he really wouldn't like the idea of the other thing, which you haven't told him: how a certain cold reality overtook you when you found the nits in your own hair, how when you called him at work to find out what time he'd be home to help you with them and he said, "I don't know; I was planning to stay a little late and look up some airfares on the Internet," you hung up and drove directly to the pharmacy and then to Gary's, where you shed your clothes in his bathroom, got in the tub, and summoned him in to do the washing.

"Massage into hair, saturating every strand," you said to Gary, not even bothering to try to strike the note of gentleness his shrinking soul always required and never got from you. "Really, Gary. Don't dick around. Just get them out."

You hated the way Gary's hands felt in your hair—tentative and ineffectual, as always—which was reassuring. You both know you've made the right decision, though sometimes other people try to tell you you haven't. You must still have feelings for each other, they say. You seem to like each other.

Lice has an odd power, you are starting to discover, to show you things about your life.

For example, right there in the tub, you had a realization, suddenly, after all these years of separating from Gary: that you will be able to go forward, to life without Gary, but you will never be able to go back. You can't get rid of the facts: that Gary watched you give birth to Katrin—propel a child out of your body, vomit, piss on the floor, bellow like an elephant; walk around afterward naked and moaning, your breasts, rock hard and blue with engorgement, bigger than his head.

You think about the lingering, romantic, newly-in-love feelings that up until now still graced the atmosphere of your home with the boyfriend; you think about their sudden loss of substantiality, their lack of fortitude. You picture them as dropouts of a boot camp run by lice.

Another of the powers of lice is that it is placing unfamiliar words in your brain. "I can *do* this," you hear yourself thinking. You've come a long way from the days of driving around, crying, with baby Katrin strapped in the backseat. It is not a comforting thought, just new information for your life: Whatever impossible, unimaginable task you are called upon to do, you can do.

- Call Tinka Potter re: PTO "Oktoberfest" Committee—get off my back

You might start to notice something: If there is a problem in your life, lice will reveal it as surely as—

Say your mother's in town, too. Say she's come to stay for two months, or as your boyfriend says, "TWO MONTHS!," which sounded, somehow, in February, over the telephone, not like the terrible idea it actually is.

Add to this the fact that you are a baker by "trade," a word your mother likes to employ to distinguish your job from other kinds of jobs, say, like hers: Professional Poet; then factor in a lice infestation. Katrin has just been sent home from school with a second round of lice—three weeks, three poisonous shampooings, thirty-six loads of laundry, and forty-two combings into the ordeal—even though you've instructed her not to take off her cap, not to undo her braided bun, not to hug, touch, or brush up against another human being until this is all over. It will seem then, in some strange way, exactly perfect—the final, brilliant brushstroke on some perverse dream masterpiece— that when you arrive home from work ("You must be *tired*," your mother says, meaning, after your long day of low-paying toil), she has made, there in your kitchen, a blueberry pie. Caved in, pallid, just like the pies of your childhood—the childhood she has come to hold against you all: you, your brother, your dead father. "Back when I was a cookie-pusher in Salt Lake," is the way she refers to that time now.

"Guess what makes my crust so flaky?" she warbles. You can see that your dish drainer's been emptied, your sink cleaned, your newspapers neatly stacked.

"Lard, Mother?" you whisper savagely, not in the mood to hear the familiar rendering (ha) of the amazing properties of lard, first part in a set piece, the second part of which features your mother as innocent shiksa newlywed, feeding lard crust to her unsuspecting Jewish mother-in-law, which makes you think of your dead father, whose hair—thick, black, curly, oily—was always a fascination to you.

"Yuck, Abby," he'd say, when you picked up his special silver-plated, soft-bristled hairbrush. You loved to smooth its bristles across your own head. "Don't touch that." Which made no sense at all: It was the same hair that tickled your face when you hugged him, that you put your hands in when you rode on his shoulders. It was your mother, you knew, who had done it—you remember the face she made when he scratched his head, as if she were watching to see if anything would fall out. Your mother had the power to turn a man against his own hair.

"Someone named Missy Bindle called," she says. "She sounded nice. Is she a friend of yours?" The question is

44

ridiculous. Maybe there will be time for friends again, sometime in the future.

Missy Bindle is the mother of the child on whose scalp the problem originally arrived at school, and she's an expert on lice now. She can often be seen holding impromptu informational sessions—outside the school at pick-up time, at the swimming pool in the afternoons, on the street downtown. Lice is never far from her mind, though Elspeth's been clean at least two months. Missy Bindle is starting to seem like one of those old guys who never got over the war.

"There's anecdotal evidence that shampooing prophylactically with Head & Shoulders twice a week is an effective deterrent," she says at the swimming pool, where the mothers have gathered, as if around an oracle.

"You have to buy a metal comb, those plastic ones are no good."

"Vinegar loosens the nits from the hair shaft, but it also interferes with the killing effects of the products."

"Clean hair repels them."

"I heard the opposite," one of the other mothers says. "That slightly dirty hair keeps them away."

You didn't have the heart to tell Missy Bindle what you'd read about the neutralizing effect of chlorine on Nix. All the little girls were swimming happily. "Why don't they just drown?" Katrin asked you. "Why can't I just hold my head underwater for five or six hours?" she asked one night when you started crying as you combed.

Did you ever think of this? If your mother gets lice, *you* are the one who's going to have to go through her hair.

She uses up all your shampoo, disregards the package instructions, shampoos several times in a row. You pray for them to obediently die. When she comes out with her head in a towel, you look at her blankly. If you asked, anyone would tell you: You have to do it. The fact of your undutifulness has never been thrown at you quite so baldly before; you have definitely begun to feel something like awe at the power of these tiny bugs to bring the ugly heart of a thing to light.

You have to hand it to her, though. After she's combed, she takes the laundry over to Gary's and does it all—yours, Katrin's, Gary's, even the boyfriend's. She offers to comb Katrin the next night, but then gets too drunk to do it. But every day till the end of her stay, she does the laundry; she vaccuums. She gives up asking careful, veiled questions, the meaning of which is, How could this have happened? She only says, "*You* kids never had lice" once; seeing your dangerous look, she changes her nuance in midstream: "Hmm, I wonder why."

She also can't wait to get out of there. She's got a side-trip to the city planned. The day before she goes, she offers to comb your hair, but when you let her, she just ruffles her fingers around your scalp randomly, asking, "Is this one? Is this one, honey? Is *this* one?"

"Never mind," you tell her. Tomorrow you will call the health center, get an answer to the question you forgot to ask: "Who combs the parents' hair?"

WHO WILL COMB YOUR HAIR?

Like your own death, this is something you should plan for before it happens. So that you don't have to find yourself sitting on the floor at eleven o'clock on a work night, feeling like a despairing princess in a fairy tale. Many have tried and failed. As a last resort, you've asked your boyfriend, but he fails, too. "Your hair's so overwhelming," he says, from where he kneels behind you. He keeps stopping his random, halfhearted combing to argue with you.

"Can't you at least fight and comb at the same time?" you say. Your butt's numb, your eyes ache, from two hours of work on Katrin's head and another hour on his.

"That's it," he says, and he wings the comb across the room. It hits the wall and its little plastic magnifying glass flies off. You begin to cry. You cry for one minute, then you get the phone book and the phone. This is the order of the people you can ask for help: almost-ex-husband, mother, boyfriend, almost-ex-husband's recently jilted girlfriend.

- strongly recommend trying to avoid getting in situation of having almost-ex-husband's recently jilted girlfriend be last-resort comber

Even if she asks repeatedly; even if she calls before anyone else knows you have them and says, "I've been there, it's awful. Let me know if there's anything I can do to help." Her daughter and Katrin are in the same class, and Elinor's case of lice seems to be indomitable. Every night, according to Lynette, the girlfriend, Elinor's short, scraggly hair is combed till "there's not one speck of *anything* in it," and every day she is sent home by the school nurse. "They must be jumping on her head from the other children," Lynette says. She starts calling every day. "I know how hard it can be to get someone to comb you out," she says. "Why don't we just set up a time?"

What if you can't avoid it? What if the momentum of lice is giving your life a shape you can only watch transmogrify grotesquely, while your real aspirations—sitting down to a well-prepared meal without a stomachache, having fifteen minutes left at the end of the day to take a bath or fold laundry—seem to have evaporated with a cold, hard finality?

Under such circumstances, you might find yourself, on a Saturday night, sitting in the bright, over-decorated living room of your almost-ex-husband's recently jilted girlfriend, having a conversation with him in your head. Cute like her, you say, about the room. You are focusing on the enormous cabbage roses on the girlfriend's living room rug, on the two sweating, warming beers you brought, which are sitting, small in the distance, on the kitchen counter beyond the wide double door.

You know before her finger even touches the stereo's Power button that you'll be listening to Jonathon Richman or African dance music. Gary's cassette player's been broken for three years, about the same amount of time as your marriage has, so he brings his CDs over to your apartment for the boyfriend to record. You don't tell Lynette that there are at least three other women with the exact micro-collection she's now asking you to choose from. You also don't tell her that the last time Gary went out with her, you asked him, "Did she wear her little headband?" and that Gary laughed, and answered, "I'm afraid so."

And she hasn't said to you, yet—woman to woman, friend to friend—the comb firmly set in your scalp, "I *told* Gary he wasn't your father and he didn't have to take care of you." She hasn't yet said, referring to your furniture that you couldn't stand to take because Katrin hates for anything to change: "Look at his *house*. Everything he has is junk. Look at the way he lives!" She also hasn't said the thing that causes you to wrinkle your eyebrows at its incomprehensibility: "I really hope Katrin didn't get lice from Elinor. She had them the day Katrin came over to play, but I didn't tell Gary because I was so mad at him."

She spreads a sheet on the floor to collect the vermin that will be raining from you; she has you sit at her feet, and she puts her small, feathery hands in your hair.

"I think I'm going to write a guide," she says. For other parents, about how to get rid of lice. "Straight talk," Lynette says firmly. You wonder what other kind she thinks she's capable of.

Missy Bindle's writing a guide, too. Why does everyone else have the good ideas? Not that you could ever write a guide, but if you did, maybe it would be something besides straight talk. The more peripheral issues, like: What if lice is the anti-missing-puzzle-piece, the thing that sends all the little pieces of your life flying irretrievably in different directions? Or if it's like secret-tarnish remover—if getting lice is the thing that rubs all the accumulated grime, the obscuring effect of everyday life, off the secrets that have been sitting there forever: You might never be able to forgive your mother, even if you try; you are a better mother than you ever thought you would be, and aren't quite sure what to do with that knowledge; you might never be ready for this divorce, even though you know it's a good idea; and another man is not the answer. What to do then. Maybe that would be a guide people could use—not like Missy's or Lynette's, but one for *after* they get rid of lice. Because—they can't know until it happens, but you know, now—life will never be the same.

One of the ironies of lice is that Gary's the only one who doesn't get them. The hub of the infestation, and he remains untouched. Probably it's because he's balding fast, but you have a moment of thinking that maybe it's his attitude. He doesn't let anyone close; maybe the lice respect that.

One day Gary feels dizzy and short of breath on the tennis court. He calls to tell you about it. "Get to the doctor," you tell him, which, uncharacteristically, he does. The doctor says he's fine. You have a combing scheduled with him for the next day. "Come at four o'clock," he says. He's found he prefers to comb in natural light, in the late afternoon, in a white plastic chair on the front porch. The comb-ee sits in a child-sized chair in front of him. "I've actually gotten sort of strangely into this," he says.

"You know my little heart attack yesterday?" Gary says. His hands have gotten much better in your hair—quick, firm, and decisive.

"My preferred method," he says, when you yelp—when he finds a hair shaft with a nit on it, he yanks it clean out of your head. You just let him. You think, maybe lice was the moment your marriage was always waiting for.

"Yeah?" you say. You were just in the middle of talking about the usual things: Katrin's schedule, her activities sign-up deadlines, which lunchbox is at whose house.

"Well, I just thought I'd go through this real quick, in case anything happens to me," he says, and he tells you the provisions of his life insurance policy and Katrin's college fund, and what to do about the mortgages, and where all the papers are to be found.

"Gary!" You don't need this in the middle of everything.

"Well," he replies.

"Don't die," you tell him, and you don't even mean: because then there won't be anybody to comb my hair, or maybe you do.

Your mother is calling every couple of days, asking after everyone's head, trying to hide the fact that she is so glad to be out of there.

"How're you holding up, sweetie?" she asks, and you think about how you will probably die without knowing why words like that have the effect of making you feel as if long fingers are raking the insides of you, trying to re-arrange things in there, screw up the order things have finally fallen into.

"Fine," you say. You don't tell her that Katrin still has lice and Gary has gone to Tulsa to visit his new girlfriend, some-one he met at a conference in some other, grown-up world where lice don't circulate. The visit was arranged before the lice trouble; you thought of asking him to change his plans, but you didn't. You were surprised by the knowledge that cornered you: You can't afford—not just yet—to risk hearing Gary say the one thing he never says to you, the thing, like the last louse left on a ravaged scalp, after which, having been rooted out, everything will change and the rest of life will begin.

"Go," you said to him. "Have a good time." You felt utterly abandoned; of course you don't tell your mother that, and you don't tell her this: You've started to see her around.

All your adult life you've dreamed her: walking down the street, unaware that you've caught her, living in your town all along and never letting you know. But lately these apparitions have stepped out of your dreams and into real life. You keep seeing her driving around town. Why haven't you ever noticed before how many sixty-year-old women there are in the world who look exactly like your mother, driving blue Accords? They never see you, and you turn away; you don't want to be seen.

Anyway, if you write a guide, put this in it. The next time one of those women drives by, don't be afraid if something happens. If one of those women in a blue Honda drives by, and you suddenly get a picture in your head, almost as if she's bumped you with a fender and caused it to pop out, don't be afraid to look at it.

You might actually consider using illustrations in your guide. Not just the usual, a magnified picture of a louse, with its actual dimensions and Latin name written underneath it, but maybe something more like this: a surprised woman who looks just like you, standing on the sidewalk watching another woman who's not her mother drive by. You might need a series of illustrations to show this. Her problem has reached monumental proportions, though it's still invisible to the outside world, and she is just about to decide to take desperate measures—beg for a prescription for the really poisonous stuff, send away for information about homeschooling, shave her head and her child's head, set fire to all their possessions, and move away to the desert—*do what she has to do*—when the problem suddenly, miraculously, eradicates itself. Not gradually, like it's supposed to—the dead bugs falling out, the tiny eggs prised from the hair shafts over hours and days with the little comb, the methodical correcting of the problem over time, which, everyone will tell you, is the one and only way you will ever be able to crawl back into your life—but all in a single, stunning instant. Hundreds, thousands of the little things jump off her head, like

- Medusa with detached snakes
- Sea monkey party
- Cartoon sweat beads
- A bunch of happy, olden-days kids (Missy Bindle says post-1970s rise in lice due to DDT ban) jumping out of trees, yelling a thousand little "Geronimo"s

leaving her like she was before (nothing like she was before?): a little light-headed, a little uninhabited, a little able to feel, whenever anyone mentions it (ask Leon: Can he draw this?), the absent itch.

THE LAST KNOWN THING

She used to walk to the end of the pier with a horseshoe crab and throw it over. Sometimes she took two—a prickly spike for each hand. Then she'd run back down the pier, across the yard to the tiny beach—it wasn't far. No matter how fast she ran, the crab would already be there, lined up along the small crescent of shore with three or four or five others, swaying under the surface of the shallow water.

They always came back to the same spot, though there was a whole big ocean—"sound," her mother said—in front of Abby's house. Abby imagined a line, like a narrow road, stretched under the water from the pier to the beach; she pictured the crabs traveling along the line. The underwater line formed a triangle with the pier and the shore, and Abby's job—carrying the crabs to the end of the pier, throwing them in, and running back for them again—reminded her of something she liked to do at school: tracing. The teacher would hand out a sheet of paper filled with dotted lines and arrows; if you moved your pencil over the lines, you could make a letter or a shape. Abby liked moving her hand over and over the same spot, making lines on top of lines, lines next to lines, lines that crossed and twisted like thread. She liked letters that closed—little *a*, little *o*, big *B*—and shapes. Triangles elbowed the space around them; circles were best—with one slow swoop she could separate outside from in, pen space: A little animal could live there. She liked the sound of tracing, too: the way a triangle went one two three, one two three, and a circle droned, swelled in the same spot every time, sounded round, like her mother's records at the end of a side. Her mother said tracing was bad; she thought Abby's teacher should just give the children blank pieces of paper and let them draw.

The crabs always looked to Abby like they were waiting for something, lined up at the edge of the shore. She'd feel a little bad, like she might be wrecking their plans, taking them to the end of the pier again. But she didn't know what else to do. She didn't know where their home was; she didn't think it was the place they kept coming back to. She couldn't imagine one anywhere along the straight-lined path they traced.

Driving Stephen to the airport makes Abby remember the crabs. Stephen's been silent since Springfield, though they haven't been fighting. Abby's three-year-old, Katrin, is sleeping in the backseat. Abby thinks of the crabs because she's thinking about happiness—she wants to ask Stephen what would make him happy. But she realizes she won't believe any answer he might give, so she ends up asking a different question, an easier one. One whose answer won't be of any practical use, she realizes, as soon as the words leave her mouth: "When was the last time you were happy?"

She knows for certain she was happy at five, when the good and bad together simply formed the landscape in which she lived. She remembers the pier, the crabs, an Indian bedspread on her mother and father's bed in the living room, her father smiling in a brown woven sweater, her mother in a raccoon coat on the roof, sweeping off snow with a broom and shouting, "God *damn* it all, God *damn* it all!" And the color of it: the gray-painted cement floor of the living room; hazy white-gray light coming through the corner windows from behind a Christmas tree; blue and green and cloudy white beach glass in a green glass jar; the gray green of her mother's stare; the green blue of a mallard's head.

"Hmmm. Happy," Stephen says, staring straight ahead at the road in front of him. It's a bleak November day; the sky is white, the trees skeletal. Abby doesn't know if this depresses Stephen as it does her—he likes New England. He grew up here, though he lives in San Francisco now. The trip to the airport is becoming habitual, part of a migratory pattern; Abby lives in Massachusetts, and for the past year and a half—since they met—Stephen's been traveling back and forth while they try to decide what to do. Each visit sends him reeling back to his coast. He seems amazed every time they fight. "I can't *believe* it," he says, the moment the tone of their discussion turns fractious. "I'm incredulous." Each time he says it, Abby has the same slightly stupid reaction; she looks at him blankly, waiting for him to explain, but he never does.

Stephen looks like he's thinking about the answer to Abby's question, but then he says, "Did I ever tell you about the day my brother's divorce was finalized?" Abby's heard the story before, but she can't remember how it ends, so she says, "No."

"The day my brother had to go to court to get the

arrangements finalized," Stephen begins; the important part—the part that Abby's forgotten—is the last line: "And our father turned to him and said, 'How come everything you touch turns to shit?' " Stephen turns to look at her, and waits a minute.

"And that's what I feel like now," Stephen says. "Like everything I touch turns to shit." Abby waits, pretends to be gauging the gravity of this, instead of wondering why she doesn't think things are so bad.

They're getting close to the airport; Abby knows that they won't work this out before he leaves. When the car stops, Katrin will wake up and they won't be able to talk anymore. Stephen will kiss Abby good-bye, and the kiss will be like always—a question and its answer, a bolt of knowing. Then he'll fly to California for two months or maybe longer this time. The kiss will make the weight and shape and meaning of the words they're about to speak changeable and elusive in Abby's memory; the memory of it will make her confused, later, on the phone.

"A time when I was happy," Stephen begins again, and hesitates. Abby braces herself—he was happy, she imagines, when he had a home with Sandra, a steady, sanguine woman, from the way he describes her, who never fought with him, and who thought his "grumpiness" (this is what he calls it, as if he's a character in a children's book—a cranky dwarf or scary bear) made him an amusing figure. "She laughed and ignored it," Stephen told Abby, looking at her skeptically. At some point Abby realized that odd images would come into her head when Stephen talked about Sandra; she pictured something dense and insulated and strangely thick around the edges, a human hotpad.

But Stephen had left Sandra. He'd left, or been left by, all the women whom Abby is now imagining him happier with. Sometimes Abby pictured Stephen's past as a line, every woman a blip along it. The blips were different-sized, but still, all small, until the last one—her. She was a big clot, a blot, a storm of activity along Stephen's line, but not the end. There, breaking through the tangle, like a train through a tunnel, was the line again, moving straight and clean and alone as before.

"I was happy when I was living in the south of France by myself, working on my second book," Stephen says. Abby tries to remember why he was alone, what women he'd been between.

"And I was pretty happy for a while after I finished *The Things That Matter*, and it got good reviews, and I was relaxing, starting to write my next book."

"When was that?" Abby asks. She thinks he was with Sandra then.

"Nineteen eighty-one," he answers. She waits. When he speaks again, it's not what she expects.

"I think," he says, looking off into the white-gray sky, "I haven't been happy since before my father died. And my back started bothering me." Ahead of them, traffic is slowing. Abby tries to think of what to say.

"So," Stephen says, after a minute, "I guess it's been a while since I was happy. What is this, bridge traffic?"

People are braking up ahead. Stephen sits up; his attention sharpens like a wary animal's. Abby brakes, too, and in a moment they've joined the slow-moving mass of cars. Stephen is peering around, trying to see the cause of the jam.

"Bridge traffic," he says again, then his voice amplifies in anger. "They've been working on this fucking thing for years." He's craning his neck, trying to look around the line of cars in front of them. Abby doesn't want to talk about the traffic jam. She has the feeling of not knowing who she's talking to when Stephen gets like this. Or she doesn't know who *he's* talking to—isolation surrounds his anger like a membrane; sometimes it seems as if there's someone in there with him.

"So," she says, "you were happy being alone and doing your work. What about the love part?

"You don't have to spare me," she adds. He stares at her a moment, trying to decide, she thinks, exactly what she's accusing him of. When he speaks, he sounds defensive.

"Oh. Right. I didn't mention love, did I? I talked about being happy working . . . living in France . . ." He's thinking.

Tracing, Abby thinks. It's something he does in difficulty: goes back again and again to find the starting point, the one moment that counts to him—the unbelievable moment in which some crucial wrong or injustice, which makes love impossible, has been done. They can fight for hours, days, and Abby will see the lie it is for him to believe whatever fragile resolution they've come to; she'll see him working backward, coming to rest—even with her finally in his arms, him in hers—on that last known thing.

"Well, I'm certainly not saying I've never been happy in love," Stephen says. "That second time I was talking about— I was with Sandra then. There was certainly a time when we weren't unhappy, when our relationship was fine." He stops to think again, calculating: "Eighty-three, eighty-two, eighty-one . . . that would've been near the beginning of the time we were together." He nods to himself. "So yeah, we would've been happy."

"Well, I didn't mean to imply . . . ," Abby says, glancing at him, but he's not looking at her. He's looking at the road ahead, the slowed traffic, with great interest, and when he speaks, it's as if he's discovered something that's going to make a difference to them.

"*I* see," Stephen says; he leans as far in her direction as his seat belt will allow. "We lose the left lane up there." He cranes to see, then he nods.

"Yep," he says. "That's it. We lose the left lane. All these cars"—he gestures, thrusts one hand, palm up, out in front of him—"have to get over *here*." The space of the front seat seems filled by Stephen. Suddenly he leans away from Abby, all the way to the other side of the car.

"Wait. Maybe we lose the right lane. I can't tell anymore." Abby's driving in the middle lane; she wants to tell Stephen that it doesn't matter.

"Is that the bridge up there? Can you see?" he asks, not taking his eyes from the situation ahead.

Abby forms sentences mentally: Yes, it's the bridge; no, I can't see it. She knows that anything she says, or asks, will be the wrong thing—will make him angry. Especially what she really wants to know: Why does this matter so much? Can't you see there's nothing you can do?

Katrin stirs in her car seat, and Abby glances back at her, feeling agitated herself. Abby wants Katrin to keep sleeping; she doesn't want her to see Stephen upset. Abby realizes for the first time, with surprise, that she feels a responsibility to keep Katrin from angry men, like she keeps her from strange dogs, scary television shows, things with the capacity to do an unknown amount of damage.

Stephen's always been gentle with Katrin. But he looks, right now, like someone Abby doesn't know. Abby pictures him, for a second, as Katrin's father; the image pains her. Then she can't shake the image, of a father, sitting there beside her: not hers—her father wasn't often angry; not

Katrin's; but someone else. She's looking at Stephen and seeing a man she's never met—someone irascible and overbearing and absolute—but is coming to know, someone she doesn't like very much.

There's no way they'll get back to their conversation, Abby sees; Stephen is completely absorbed by what's happening on the road.

"My God," he's saying, "this *isn't* bridge traffic." The road has curved, and he can see into the distance. "We're not even near it—this is all just construction." Finally, he turns to look at Abby. She glances at him, careful to keep all expression off her face, then looks back at the road.

"It's construction," Stephen says again. "They've got the right lane *and* the left lane blocked off up there." He shakes his head; his face is in a deep frown. "This is bad," he says, and he's still looking at her, as if he's waiting for her to say something.

"We'll still be on time," Abby says. He looks at her blankly for a minute, then glances at his watch.

"Yeah." He sounds impatient, as if she doesn't get it, as if she's distracting him.

If she could only take him somewhere. The idea surges by; she's left with just the slipped skin of words.

All the gray and white and bleakness has her thinking of the little house on the Long Island Sound. It had been the carriage house of a larger, more elegant place; its drive-way dropped off the larger house's driveway at the end of a dead-end road and widened abruptly into a disorderly convergence of gravel and dirt, cement and dirty stucco, water and pier and sand and grass and sky.

That house had felt like the end of something, Abby thinks. It had been a place things came to: the horseshoe crabs that swam, of all the places they could go under the dark water of the Sound, to *her* beach, the beach that was in front of *her* house. One night when there had been company, and a storm outside, Abby's mother had rolled up towels and put them in front of the door. It was going to flood, she said. The grown-ups had been drinking and talking and laughing, and Abby had been happy and excited; she'd asked to put on her bathing suit, because the big ocean out front was going to roll in—like a road, she thought—to her living room.

Abby's mother, in the house on the Sound, wouldn't break her stare when Abby asked a question. "Mmm," she'd say—the sound between yes and no; often, the sound before anger.

Abby thinks of something Stephen told her once: When he was little, he liked to ask grown-ups questions that he already knew the answers to. "Not to show off," he explained. "I'd just listen. There was something I really liked about knowing what the answer to a question was going to be."

She thinks of the way Stephen's words sometimes flashed dangerously across a corner of her, like a hand raised against her; the way hers sometimes seemed to disappear in him to some place she hadn't meant them to go, some place she didn't even know about except for the way his eyes, opaquing in unsurprise, looked out from there.

If she could only take him somewhere.

There was a place, Abby thinks she remembers, where things piled up and nothing left: anger and fear and loss and love, forgiveness washing over in daily tides. There was a place, she liked to imagine, that didn't seem to be continuously, without purpose, radiating its own essential elements into the atmosphere.

The traffic begins to ease after about a quarter of a mile. Stephen relaxes as they speed back up to sixty. He settles again in his seat and stares out the window. After a minute he asks, "Were we talking about anything? Before all that?"

Abby hesitates. They're about ten miles from the airport; she's feeling jangly, on a dangerous edge. "No," she answers.

There's still construction, but traffic runs smoothly. Stephen watches the road, turning his head to look at the configurations of barrels, the earthmovers and backhoes, the orange-suited men alongside the freeway. He's calm now. The construction doesn't seem to bother him as long as he can see the open stretch of gray in front of him. Abby thinks, from the way he looks, that if she asked what he was thinking right now, he'd say, "Nothing." She's thinking that the road is ugly. This seems like a stunning piece of knowledge to Abby, irreducible as a rock: This place is so incredibly ugly. The smooth, hard surface of new road, the dangerous-looking concrete divider that runs up the middle of it, the slabs of uninstalled concrete that line its edges haphazardly, the machinery, the plowed-up dirt all around: That's the fact of this place. The landscape that it's replaced isn't even imaginable to Abby.

She can't believe that people are expected to do this: She can't believe she's driving this road, barreling, thoroughly harrowed, through a corridor of concrete with her child in the backseat.

Ahead, a huge machine—a kind she's never seen before—moves slowly down the emergency lane. She doesn't know what about it frightens her. Stephen is looking, too. It's black, with arms; it crawls and steams. Men, emerging and disappearing in the steam, ride in various places on it, or walk alongside. While Abby's looking at the machine, she drives underneath the first airport exit sign. Suddenly, makeshift signs announcing the exit, and a detour, start appearing on her right.

"What's this?" Abby says.

"Detour," answers Stephen, peering at the signs. The signs say it's a quarter-mile to the exit, which seems wrong to Abby. The real exit is at least a mile, she knows; she can't see anything up ahead but a lot of orange and white barrels. There's a diamond-shaped orange sign, bigger than the others, coming up; Abby can't read it yet but she knows it's going to give her some confusing instruction that she'll have to instantaneously carry out.

"What's that say?" she asks Stephen, but he can't read it, either; then it becomes clear to both of them at once.

"Unfamiliar patterns," they read aloud, in identical puzzled tones; they laugh at the unison.

"Yeah? And?" says Abby, and Stephen says, "Never saw that one before." Then suddenly the exit is right there—a narrow passageway through the mess of barrels. The road curves sharply to the right; Abby has to brake and pull the wheel. Stephen braces himself; they both lean, rigid and mute—parallel statues—against the centrifugal force of the car.

Abby brings the car out of the curve and merges onto the airport road. She glances back at Katrin, who, surprisingly, hasn't woken.

"Shit," says Abby, after a minute. "Jesus." Stephen is looking at her. He puts his hand on her knee, rubs her thigh. She's suddenly angry.

"That's a *stupid* fucking sign," she says, almost shouting. "Unfamiliar patterns! What the fuck is that supposed to mean? How about 'Slow'? 'Exit Three Feet'?"

"How about: 'We've created a lot of confusion here and we don't know what to tell you but we thought we needed a sign?' " says Stephen. It makes Abby smile. "How about," he continues, " 'Something mysterious to contemplate in the moments before your certain death?' "

"God," says Abby, "what a stupid way to die that would be." Stephen is nodding his head. He wants to be with her, she thinks.

"*Here*, in this place," she says, and he looks around as if to see what she's talking about.

EXACTLY THE SIZE OF LIFE

When Abby dreams about Stephen, the two of them are always traveling. Abby and Stephen met on a raft trip in the wilderness. She'd come to Colorado from Massachusetts, he from San Francisco. It was the first time Abby had been away from her eighteen-month-old, Katrin; her marriage had been about to end.

In one dream, Stephen's car develops four flat tires while he waits outside Abby's house. She keeps having to run back inside for things she's forgotten: her keys, her sweater, Katrin's sweater, Katrin. In another, a large, broken piece of iron machinery sits abandoned in the middle of the shallow, rocky river they're traveling down. It blocks their way completely. Abby can't tell what kind of machine it is, but it's fascinating: pretty, somehow, and oddly saddening. It looks like an antique, maybe something left by the pioneers, Abby thinks in the dream.

Their first trip down a river had been wonderful, literally: a series of delighted astonishments in each other. The boats had gone into the water in Colorado and come out in Utah; Abby's sense of where, exactly, is now vague. She had politely declined to look at the maps the men on the trip were constantly proffering. She would hold a map in her hands as one or another of them hovered over her, pointing to a spot on it, and she would try not to listen: She didn't want to hear how far they were from the put-in point or the take-out point, how far they'd come in a day, what famous explorers had been where, where in relation they were to Salt Lake City or Grand Junction or Green River.

After they'd taken the boats out of the river and loaded the cars and started home, Stephen had unfolded a map and pointed out a two-and-a-half-inch section of green line to her. "See?" he'd said. "This is where we just were." He was being sentimental, Abby knew, but she only said, "Mmm," and glanced without focusing. To the east of them, still visible in the distance, was the notch of the canyon they'd emerged from half an hour before. Beyond the canyon was the river. Abby had been watching the notch as they drove—watching the wide, deep V narrow and shorten, filling itself in, as the car changed direction. Soon, Abby knew, though she could never figure out how this happened, it would become part of the level surface of the high desert on which they drove.

There had been a second trip, too; it had been different. It was a different river, and Abby and Stephen had been together, though not often in the same place, for nine months. Another difference, Abby thought—though no one else had said anything—was something that happened on the way to the river.

Abby and Stephen and Stephen's brother Jamie had arrived in southern Utah the night before everyone else. They'd camped that night, and in the morning, Jamie, who'd been there before, drove them around to places he knew. They were on their way, finally, to meet the others at the river, when Jamie made one final detour, to a place called Goosenecks State Park.

"There it is," he said, when they were still quite far away. It didn't look like much from what Abby could see— a small concrete building, some picnic tables, a guardrail, and a couple of RVs sitting on top of the flatness at the end of the long, straight road. She didn't know why they'd come to this place. When they reached the end of the road, Jamie got out of the car and strode, ahead of Abby and Stephen, to the guardrail and stood looking out.

"Goosenecks, all right," he said, not taking his eyes from the view as they walked over to join him. There, in front of them, where nothing had been before, was a winding gap in the earth where a river had carved through in a series of impossibly clean, impossibly tight loop-shaped turns. A thousand, fifteen hundred feet down, at the bottom of the canyon, lay a flat, brown band of water. It looked motionless from that height. A raft carrying four people, tiny but clearly visible, passed from shadow into sunlight.

"The San Juan," said Jamie. He pointed to a spot right below them. "That's where we'll be on Tuesday."

And Abby had been suddenly, momentarily angry at Jamie for the spark of shock, and the unmistakable twinge of disappointment she'd felt: She knew she wouldn't be able to forget, down there in what she'd been thinking of as the wilderness, that above her ran a network of roads and towns and ranches; that someone she didn't know might stand looking down from this spot on Tuesday and see her, traveling like a tourist, between two not-very-distant points on a river.

But Abby *had* almost forgotten; there was a world at the bottom of the canyon—river, rock, heat, silence—that made what lay beyond the cliff rims unimaginable. If it hadn't been for one day, she would have forgotten completely.

Jamie had wanted to go for a hike he'd read about in his guide book, on an old prospecting trail that switched back and forth from the river to the top of the canyon wall. They'd taken the boats out of the water early on the third day and made camp on the river bank near the start of the trail. It had been deadeningly hot. Everyone had lain around in whatever shade they could find, drinking soda and waiting for the afternoon to wane. They hadn't waited long enough, though—it was still too hot when they started up the trail in shifts.

Afterward, they'd laughed at themselves; "Hike from hell," someone said that night at supper. "The god-damn Honaker Trail."

Abby and Stephen hadn't even made it to the top.

They'd been the last ones to start out for the hike. They'd sat under a tamarisk bush after the others had gone, waiting for the heat to abate. Abby had been reading; Stephen was leaning back next to her with his eyes closed. They hadn't been getting along well this time. They seemed to be constantly bumping against each other and spinning away, only to reconnect jarringly, bruising at each new point of contact. It reminded Abby of something: Every once in a while, when the boats would float near one another on the wide, flat stretches of river, the occupants of one, or both, would try to grab hold of the other, by ropes and lines, by an oar if it was offered, by each other's hands. The aim was to hold on, or lash the rafts together and float like that—a ponderous, unnavigable mass of rubber and bodies and provisions, spinning slowly downstream.

What surprised Abby every time was how difficult it was to ease the boats parallel—it was much more difficult than it looked, from any distance, like it was going to be. The boats' tranquil, weightless glide on flat water always belied the force with which they hit. There was a moment each time—a certain distance, almost just exactly too small to act in—at which the swollen gunwales of the approaching boat suddenly looked serious, not soft and yielding at all, capable of inflicting a little damage; even the most languid passenger would brace him or herself, pull in arms and legs, sit up and grab a rope.

Stephen and Abby had been sitting on a little rise facing the river. Suddenly there was a whoop of laughter, some activity in the water; Abby put down her book to watch. It was Janet, the trip's leader, and her husband, Paul. They'd walked upriver a few hundred yards, and now they were riding the current down—two shining, smiling heads, two bobbing orange life vests, two pairs of outstretched arms, floating past.

"Look," Abby said. Stephen opened his eyes and watched for a moment, without expression, then closed them again.

"They're having fun."

Stephen opened his eyes again, but he still didn't say anything. Abby looked at his severe profile: adamant cheekbones, jutting jaw, brow like a shelf. His mouth was fixed in a slight, unconscious frown. She got up and put her book down in her chair. "I'm going in," she said to him. "Want to float?"

"No," he said, closing his eyes again.

Abby found a vest and walked upriver, following the bank out of sight. Stepping into the water, she felt relief from the oppressive heat, and, as she struggled against the current to walk out to where she could float without crashing against the rocky river bottom, a sudden, expansive loneliness and fear. The river, without another person in it, seemed to have changed scale. The force of the current was so much stronger than it looked. It was hardly possible, in the cumbersome life vest, to do anything but head straight down. She was doing something dangerous, Abby thought. Then she thought of Janet and Paul, bobbing and smiling, paddling ineffectually, bumping into each other and laughing.

The river carried her swiftly. There was Stephen already on the right, leaning back in his chair with his eyes closed. Abby started to swim for shore, awkward in the bulky life vest. She reached the bank forty yards downriver from Stephen. He seemed to be sleeping, she saw, as she walked up the beach toward him. She stopped and stood for a minute, looking down at him. He didn't open his eyes. She could feel the heat starting to bloom again, as if from underneath the surface of her skin.

When Abby floated past the second time, Stephen was gone. She struggled out of the river again and walked up to a spot on the beach near their empty chairs. She took off her life vest and sat down at the edge of the water. She was waiting for Stephen, she knew, feeling irritated at herself. Maybe he'd just left for a minute—she could picture him in the vicinity: filling a water bottle over at the kitchen area, chatting with whomever was there; or at their sleeping spot, rummaging through his bag for something he'd suddenly needed—a clean T-shirt, a book, some aspirin. But she could also picture him headed away from camp; she could see the resoluteness in his stride intensify as he reached the start of the trail, his weight shifting forward, his legs pushing down, as if the trail were rising up to resist him.

Someone was moving up the beach toward her. It was Stephen. He was carrying a water bottle. Around his neck was a pair of binoculars. He was walking slowly, not looking at her. When he reached her he stood for a minute, then he said, "I'm going up the trail. Do you want to go?"

"No," Abby said.

Stephen looked at her for another moment, then turned and left. Abby stood up, and walked slowly over the rise and down the path to their sleeping spot. She rubbed sunscreen onto her face, put on sunglasses and a hat and socks and shoes; then she walked slowly back down the path through camp, and beyond it, past all the clumps of sleeping bags and tents, in the direction she'd seen the others leaving earlier.

She couldn't see Stephen, and she didn't know where to look: She couldn't tell what direction the trail could possibly take up the steep hill. The path in front of her was clear, though—dry and sandy, and marked with recent footprints. Abby followed it. After a while it veered to the left, and as it did, Stephen came into sight.

About fifty yards ahead of her, the trail started to rise up the sandy foot of the hill; a little way beyond that, it turned sharply and began to ascend in a steep traverse. That's where Stephen was; she watched him turn the corner, disappearing to the waist behind a large rock, then reemerging, suddenly seeming much farther above her than he'd just been.

Abby stopped moving. She didn't want him to see her hurrying to catch up with him; she didn't want to watch him, even for a tiny, involuntary moment, deciding whether or not to wait. She could walk like this happily, she thought: alone, looking at her feet, the trail, the rocks along its sides; glimpsing Stephen, or parts of him—just flashes—now and then above her.

Abby realized that she'd forgotten to bring water. But it was too late to go back—she'd lose Stephen. It was hot enough, she calculated, that there was a point at which, if she hadn't caught up with him, she'd be in trouble. There was time to think about it, she told herself. She knew she would keep walking; she saw that fact as if from outside of herself.

When she looked up again, toward the direction he'd been moving in, Stephen was gone. Her first thought was that he'd spotted her and stepped up his pace. But then she did see him. He'd stopped at the switchback, and was standing with his binoculars up to his face, looking in the direction of camp. Abby had been astonished, then almost at the same moment, not surprised at all—she'd felt something weighty and precarious inside her shift damagingly into place. He was scanning slowly: the beach, the camp, the bushes—she wasn't mistaken. But he wasn't going to see her; the binoculars were aimed beyond her and over her head.

She picked up her pace. Now she was walking toward him, in front of him, underneath him. She imagined herself back at camp—a tiny woman within the ellipse of his sight, wandering desultorily here and there; kneeling by her river bag, pulling things out, putting them back in; touching something of his; sitting down in the shade next to the other men. She imagined, with an odd empathy for Stephen, the shock and disorientation he'd feel if, angling the glasses, he caught sight of the real her coming toward him, blurry and lumbering; large unidentifiable parts of her filling his frame, jerking toward him faster than he could focus. She somehow imagined him—though this wouldn't, of course, be true—not having the presence of mind to put the glasses down.

She thought Stephen would hear her as she drew closer. She wanted him to, now. She wanted him to notice her from just the right distance, silent, climbing gracefully, unaware of being watched; and from the right angle—

oblique. A cheekbone angling out from under her hat, a plane of brown thigh. Things she knew he liked to see.

She passed to the side of him; he was still looking for her. Abby was almost at the bend in the trail. She could have heard him move; she wondered why he didn't hear her. Then he lowered the binoculars—she was just at the threshold of his consciousness. She'd felt a little bit of shame at her enjoyment of the moment: of the knowledge that he'd turn now, with a slight delay, like a baby, to examine what it was he was seeing.

He'd been surprised. "Hi," he said, sounding uncomfortable, "you're here," then nothing else. She hadn't said anything, either, then or later; she'd never told him that the picture—of him standing on the mountain with his binoculars—had become indelible; that she harbored it like knowledge, carried it around like an answer she just might find the question to.

Stephen walked in front of Abby, not talking much, squinting up toward the top of the mountain. He was, she knew, feigning a better mood than he felt. When they'd seemed fairly near the top, something had caught his eye.

"Look," he said, stopping. He pointed at a rim of rock a fair distance above them. "There's Linda and Lee and Terry. I think they're at the top."

"I don't see them," Abby said. Stephen took a few steps back down toward her, offering her his water bottle. Abby took the water and sat down on a low rock on the side of the trail. Stephen sat down, too, on a rock that was too near hers; their thighs touched. Abby was still looking where Stephen had pointed. "Where do you think they went?" she asked. "I wonder what's up there."

"There's a parking lot up there," Stephen said.

Abby laughed unenergetically. "I wouldn't doubt it," she said. "That would be perfect. The good old Honaker Memorial Parking Lot."

"Really," he said. "I think there's a parking lot at the top." Abby looked at Stephen closely; he didn't seem to be kidding. "I thought I heard Jamie say that," he said. "There's a road up there, anyway. Lee took his running shoes."

Abby had waited for a minute, then said, carefully, because she knew her tone was going to sound wrong, "Why are we doing this?"

Stephen had seemed a little annoyed. "I don't know," he'd said. "To do it. To see the view from the top."

Finally, Abby had declined to go on. She found a rock that cast enough shade to sit in and told Stephen that she didn't mind waiting while he went up. She was surprised when he said he didn't want to go, either, a little suspicious that he'd hold it against her later. But he'd shrugged when she asked, "Are you sure?" and said, "I guess I don't really want to see a parking lot, either."

They'd sat there awhile longer, taking in the view.

They were high above the canyon floor. But it was unspectacular—confusingly so. Abby knew that if she saw a picture of this place, she'd think it was beautiful. But she'd felt as if something was being lost—some middle place she wanted to see was diminishing exactly as fast as she looked for it, like a hole dug next to the beach filling itself with watery mud.

Across from her, the other side of the canyon had changed. Or rather, it had stopped changing: The view, which she'd been watching to see how it gave way to each new configuration, had become fixed, and its composition—drab strata of fractured rock, dirt, and brush—seen from straight on, took on more interest. She couldn't believe, looking across, that they were climbing a canyon wall just like that one. It looked vertical, unnegotiable. It was strange to know that her eyes were deceiving her—that if she were at the other side of the canyon, looking for a way up, there would be handholds, footholds, animal trails, room for a person on the ledges of rock and dirt.

They descended the trail without talking much, concentrating on where they were putting their feet on the loose rocks and, like parents policing cranky children on a car trip, trying to stave off irritable exhaustion.

"Ice water," Abby had called to Stephen.

"Ice water with lemon," he'd said, not looking back. "Seltzer."

"With ice. Root beer. A&W, in a frosty mug. Chocolate milk shake with a side of ice water."

"Cold water from the hose."

They'd almost made it down without damage. Their camp came into view, though they were still deceptively far away. There was something strange about looking down on the boats and the tents, and the others who hadn't hiked, and were sitting in beach chairs reading, or swimming in the river. There was something about watching and approaching at the same time. Abby was paying attention to the size of things: It seemed important to her, suddenly, not to miss the exact moment when things became life-sized.

The landscape of camp—the individual outposts of tents and bags and ground cloths, the central kitchen area, the toilet, the sandy paths that connected all of them, and the people: There was a moment, Abby knew, when they would no longer be far away, when it would all become exactly the size of life. And before that, a long moment—a series of moments—when she wouldn't be sure.

"It looks like they got everything set up," Abby had called to Stephen. He was ahead of her, striding, as much as he could, on the path of shifting rocks. The distance between them made casual conversation pointless, Abby realized, a moment too late.

"What?" Stephen had said, stopping to look at her.

She gestured with her head down at the camp. "It looks like they've got everything set up already."

He'd looked at her for a second, then looked down at camp and nodded. She'd caught up with him, but just as she'd stopped, and was folding her arms to stand next to him, he'd turned and started walking again.

"There's Janet," Abby said, though Stephen could see everything she could. She didn't know what edge of defiance made her want to trace the scene below them out loud, like reading instructions from a difficult diagram. "There's our stuff," she said. "I didn't know we were so far away." She couldn't tell, from the back of Stephen's head, what he was looking at—whether he was looking at anything. "I wonder who that is, all the way over there. Kind of close to the toilet. They probably don't know it yet."

"Where's the toilet?" Stephen said, looking up.

"Over there," said Abby, pointing at the red metal box near some trees at the edge of camp.

"Where?" Stephen said. He'd stopped again. Abby got right next to him and pointed; her face was almost touching his.

"There," she said. There was nothing else near where she was pointing. "In those trees. About fifty feet to the right of where Janet's standing. Toward the river."

"*Where?*"

Abby looked at Stephen, surprised. He was looking down at where she was pointing, glowering, as if he were angry at something in the air out in front of him.

"There," Abby said. "See Janet, right there?" She pointed at Janet, who stood at the edge of camp, in plain sight, directly in front of them and down, shaking out an enormous electric-blue ground cloth.

"No," Stephen had said icily. "No, I don't see Janet."

Months later, Abby had thought of something: On the rafts, those who weren't rowing were supposed to watch for rocks in the river and point them out to the oarsmen, using the clock system.

"Janet at about one o'clock," she could have said to Stephen, and he would have looked directly to the spot; he wouldn't have had to look at Abby's face, or at her insistent outstretched arm, with annoyance, as if it were the embodiment of a malicious lie.

Abby hadn't been good at the clock system. She'd made Jamie angry more than a few times, forgetting: She'd turn to him and point stupidly out at the water, knowing she wasn't supposed to say, simply, "Rock," but unable, in the moment, to perform the mental translation. There it would be, or there a bunch of them would be—the real objects always fought off the picture she was supposed to have, of a clock superimposed on the whole scene. When she looked around, she'd see a lot of clocks, floating above the surface of the water, each one with a rock, dead on, at twelve o'clock.

————

But Abby hadn't thought of the clocks. She'd lowered her arm and said, "Well, Stephen, I'm not sure how else to approach this."

"Forget it," he'd said, and he'd turned and started down the trail again.

Abby had stayed a moment more, looking down at Janet, who'd finished laying out her ground cloth and now stood with her hands on her hips, surveying her site; Abby had wished that Janet would look up and see her, so she could wave.

After the hike, Stephen had apologized to Abby for being grouchy. She'd been sitting at the edge of the water; he walked over and handed her a warm Diet Pepsi.

"This was all I could find in the drag bag," he said, sitting down next to her in the still-hot sand. Her angle—low down to the river, the wall of the canyon across from her filling her vision—was making her claustrophobic. She lay back on the sand, her knees bent, her feet in the water, so that she was looking at canyon rim and sky.

She was thinking about the first trip. In the car on the way home, her mind had floated in and out of the continual conversation Jamie and Stephen had been having: Was Hell's Half-Mile before or after the confluence? Had they passed the Yampa on the third or the fourth day? What was the name of the campsite where the chunk of canyon wall fell, across the river from them, early one morning?

She had felt her memories of the place begin to encircle her. The facts had already started dropping out; images and sensations had been gathering around her, out of sequence, out of scale, in a way that would have perturbed Stephen, she thinks now, if he'd known.

She could hear the rock falling—a splintery, tumbling explosion and its high-pitched echo. The pale wall opposite had been reddening in a band at the top, with the sunrise. They'd swum in a pool under a shelf of yellowish limestone, then sat naked in the sun. The Yampa had been broad, flat, shallow, still, glistening, where it joined the Green.

She knew the kinds of things Stephen remembered. He'd told them to her lovingly, over and over again. He didn't know that she didn't like to hear them.

On the second night of the first trip, he'd recount, they'd camped at Limestone Canyon, river left. Dinner had been chicken alla puttanesca; dessert, chocolate fondue; he thought she'd been looking at him from across the fire. On the third night (Jones Hole, river right, trout meunière, green beans, baklava) they'd kissed for the first time.

He'd brought his map and some photographs with him the first time he'd visited Abby in Massachusetts.

"Look at this," he said. He was holding a photograph that someone had taken of her on the trip. She'd been standing in a purple shirt with the sleeves rolled up, the river in front of her; her head had been turned, squinting, toward the camera.

"I remember you standing there," Stephen said. "Like a river goddess. My perfect woman." Abby didn't remember, but she could tell, looking at the picture, that she'd been turned in skeptical annoyance at whichever man was aiming the camera at her.

"But I can't figure out where this would have been," Stephen had said. He had the map out, and a pen, and he was trying to make her help him remember every place they'd stopped, for swimming or hiking, or lunch, so that he would know exactly where the picture had been taken. There were already some felt-tip dots on the map, she saw—one black, two blue, a red. The section where they'd traveled—the short line of river with the dots on either side—looked clean and neat to Abby, like a healed incision. She'd let her eyes shift to the edges of the map, the blank periphery of unpopulated desert.

If she had a map, Abby thinks, she'd be uncharting it now—undoing direction, getting rid of every line that connected one thing to another. She'd travel backward, gathering in what she could save: a wedge of night sky in the dark V of a canyon, a hand coming toward her hair.

There'd been a day on the first river that Abby had almost forgotten about; it was after she'd met Stephen, but before she knew him. The boats had stopped—someone had wanted to take pictures from the shore. Stephen and Abby had been on different boats. His had pulled out on one side of the river and hers on the other.

The shore on Abby's side had been too small for exploring; there was nothing to do but wait there along it. The others on her side had been lying in the sand—sunning, reading. Abby had walked a few yards away from them, to the end of the beach, and climbed onto a big, high rock. She'd been bored but content; she was staring idly down at the water that darkened around the base of the rock when she realized she was looking at fish—lots of them, feeding. Their bodies floated under the water, waiting, perfectly still; only the open circles of their mouths, pulsing very slightly, like someone trying to speak, broke through the surface.

Abby had watched the fish for a long time, fascinated and a little repulsed. There was something raw and painful in the way the long, dark shapes of them seemed to hang suspended from their own gasping mouths. When she'd finally looked up she had seen, with surprise and a little bit of pleasure—and surprise in her pleasure, because she hadn't known yet that she liked him—Stephen, sitting on a rock almost exactly across from her. He was facing downriver, his gangly limbs drawn together in front of him, a collection of angles.

He hadn't been looking at her, but he turned just then and met her gaze for a moment. He began to turn away—shyly, or politely, Abby had thought, and she'd raised her arm suddenly in easy greeting; it was a gesture quite unlike her. They'd smiled at each other; he'd raised his arm back. The roar of the river between them had been too loud for anything to be said.

INSECTS IN AMBER

Katrin's afraid of the killer clam. But she's fascinated, too. She edges closer, sucking her thumb and staring, pulling Abby with her; Abby knows that in a moment Katrin will turn urgently, grab for Abby's clothes, and say, "Uppie me! Uppie me!" in a tone—equal measures of panic and trust—that will make Abby momentarily, stabbingly sad.

Stephen's been gone three months; he's not coming back, and the smallest things—snagging her hair accidentally on a hedge and feeling the twigs brushing through; touching her lips to Katrin's skin for too long a moment;

catching a glimpse of herself, dull and extinguished, in a downtown window—can make her sad now.

Abby watches Katrin's fear with interest. Right now Katrin wants to get closer to the clam, but she's afraid to walk and look at the same time. She averts her face and takes a few tiny steps forward, then she stops and looks. After a moment she turns her face sideways again and takes a few more steps.

Katrin's right on target, according to the child-rearing books. She wants a penis ("Right on the top of my head!" she tells Abby); she's afraid of going down the bathtub drain; she wants to know if every old thing—her grandfather, the house, a moldy lump of cheese in the refrigerator—is about to die.

Abby's made the mistake of telling Katrin she misses Stephen. There'd been a lapse in communication between Abby and Katrin's father, Gary, from whom Abby is separated. Abby hadn't been aware, at first, of Katrin's new interest in death. One day when Katrin caught her crying, Abby, unable to think of the right lie, had said, simply, "Well, honey, I'm sad because I miss Stephen." She hadn't anticipated Katrin's string of questions.

"Did he go away?" Katrin asked. "But he's coming back?"

"No," Abby had answered. "He's probably not." Katrin had said something then that puzzled Abby.

"You mean he just-appeared? Did he die?"

Later, Abby found out that Gary had been trying to explain to Katrin what happened when a person died. "They just sort of disappear," he'd told her. "They go away and they don't come back." First, though, he told her—it was fortunate, Abby thought, that Katrin had asked Gary and not her, because she would have forgotten this part—the person had to get very old. Of course, Katrin had asked Abby, "Was Stephen really, really old?"

The clam isn't actually alive; it's just a shell, sitting on a display pedestal between two fish tanks. Abby hadn't even noticed it at first—she'd been looking at the fish tanks, wondering what seemed odd about them.

"This is a mean clam, right?" Katrin says. "It'll make you die?" Abby, looking from the chipped, grizzled shell to the plaque on the wall, is startled at her daughter's intuition, until she remembers that Katrin's been to the museum before, with Gary. *The clam's name is unfairly earned. Careless divers have had their limbs caught between its heavy valves and drowned.*

Abby feels weary at the thought of trying to explain to Katrin. "This clam's not going to hurt you, sweetie," she says.

"Why?" says Katrin.

When alive, its visceral mass weighed 25 lbs.

Abby pictures her arms extending, palms up—the gesture of someone waiting to be handed something.

Imagine its body, she wants to say to Katrin. It would be heavy and slippery and alive. She feels one palm sink, as if under weight, the other rise in response to its newly discovered weightlessness.

"What does it look like?" she knows Katrin would ask. "Is it scary?" Abby realizes she has no idea what the clam would look like; no idea, even, whether she can hold twenty-five pounds in one hand.

"Why is it not going to hurt me?" Katrin asks insistently. *This animal appeared 25 million years ago.*

Abby's suddenly figured out what's wrong with the fish tanks: One's murky, and the other's clear. It must be intentional, she thinks; she wonders why.

"Why do you think you were so in love with Stephen?" Abby's friend Diana had asked her, one raw and cold day the week before. They'd been on a walk, on the wooded roads behind the college, just rounding the big curve that opened out onto the one real view of their route. Abby had been thinking how she hated the spot—she'd never gotten used to the northeastern landscape, the prospect of her married life. The sky that was so gray white so many months of the year, the mud, the sidewalk-less narrow streets, the way the ridges that ringed the valley looked in winter—their leafless trees, straight and discrete and repeating, like obsessively drawn marks, revealing everything.

Abby had felt far away from Diana; you don't understand it, she'd wanted to say.

"Was it because he was so different from Gary?"

Abby had been annoyed at the question's simplicity. Gary was kind and responsible, a wonderful father. He'd been the first boyfriend to be nice to Abby in her life. She'd quit her waitressing job in Boston and moved to western Massachusetts with Gary when he got his job at the college. Seven years later, when Abby was eight months pregnant, they'd gotten married at town hall with no guests and no witnesses.

They'd separated easily when Abby met Stephen. "It's good for you to have someone to talk to," Gary had said. Abby had moved into a room half a mile down the road until they could figure out what to do.

Stephen was a novelist. He'd been between projects when Abby met him. He had lots of free time. He carried his belongings in two duffel bags between friends' houses and house-sits; Abby had had thirteen different addresses for him in the two years she'd known him.

When Stephen came to visit from the West Coast, Abby would leave Katrin with Gary, and she and Stephen would repair to various dark places—Abby's bedroom, guest rooms in the houses of Stephen's scattered East Coast friends, the trails in the woods behind the campus where Gary taught. They'd walk there next to the river at night, or burn candles in the kitchen and cook, late, after Abby's roommate had gone to bed; they'd stay up all night, as if they could line each day with another, more real, one.

They'd passed the word "real" continually back and forth between them; now Abby can't think of how they'd meant it.

"No," Abby says in answer to Diana's question, still irritated. "It's not just that Stephen was different from Gary." She makes an effort to speak in the past tense. "I don't know why I was in love with Stephen."

Katrin is running in circles in the Vertebrate Gallery; Abby can hear her squeaky, staccato footsteps; she can picture Katrin exactly—her headlong inclination, her arms held up and out to the sides—though she's not in sight.

Abby picks up Katrin's coat and her own, their scarves and mittens and Katrin's hat, and walks toward the gallery. Framed through the open door she can see dark linoleum, cool gray light, and the bones of something big rising toward the ceiling. Katrin, a small flare of color and flesh and activity, runs past. Abby feels surprise, as she often does, catching sight of Katrin from a distance, that this big, long-limbed child is hers. She can no longer picture Katrin folded inside her body.

The last time Stephen visited, he'd gone to see his mother in Connecticut first. Abby had driven down to pick him up. When she got there, Stephen was in the living room with his friend Bill, watching a baseball game on TV. Stephen's mother sat next to them, reading magazines.

Bill was a childhood friend of Stephen's who was also in town for the day. He'd come up from New York to shop for headstones for his parents' graves. Stephen had gone with him.

In the middle of the game, Bill had called home to talk to his kids before they went to bed. Abby, leaning her head back against Stephen's chest, watched Bill through the open kitchen door. She could see him talking and smiling; she could hear his voice change, get quieter and more serious, when his wife came on. She heard him say something about a doctor's appointment, ask Mary whether she'd taken the afternoon off work, make a sympathetic clucking sound.

"We've got to be together," Stephen had said to her later that night. He was holding her head, looking right in her eyes, and she'd had some vague, puzzling feeling of unease, like she'd had when she was a child and an uncontrollable hoarder of the things people gave her—Halloween candy that she wouldn't eat until it was old and stale; picture postcards that she never sent and wouldn't put up on her bulletin board because she didn't want to make thumbtack holes in them; the polished rocks her grandmother sent her from the Southwest that she kept safe under their white rectangle of cotton inside their box in her dresser.

She had looked around the darkened room that night as

if she might see something—a pocket, a space, a safe place in which to hoard Stephen's words just the way they were right then: issued big and real into the air around them.

"I'm going to write a story," Stephen said to Abby the next day. They'd been on their way back to Massachusetts, driving toward Abby's house. "About yesterday. About Bill, and looking for the headstones, and spending time with my mother." He smiled then—a simple, heedless smile Abby never liked to see. "And you. It's going to be about me, and mortality, and you."

Abby's surprised that Katrin isn't afraid of the big bones. Probably it's because they learn about dinosaurs at day care, see them, tiny and colorful and smiling, all the time.

In front of Abby, in a glass-covered case recessed into the wall, is a display of small skeletons. "Look at this one," she says, though Katrin's already on her way to the other side of the room. " 'Reptile-like mammals,' " she reads aloud. They look like funny dogs.

There's a low plastic dinosaur footprint next to the display of large bones; Katrin runs over and scrambles into it. Abby feels some exigency she can't identify, though it seems to originate in her sadness as she looks down at her daughter, small and perfect, smiling up at her from the hollow plastic impression.

"Listen to this," Abby says. She doesn't know why it seems important. " 'Ed-a-pho-saurus.' He has a sail on his back." The bones rise delicate and comb-like from the spine, ascending to a crest, then descending, in perfect, pleasing steps.

" *'Its function is unknown,'* " she reads, though Katrin isn't listening.

She moves to the next case. "Look, Katrin," she says, and her voice sounds strange, tinged with some unexpected tenderness, or pity. " *'Eryops Megacephalus.'* " The skeleton has an oversized head at the end of a delicate spine, short legs, a large blind hole for an eye. Abby imagines something shuffling obtusely, low to the ground, following its own blunt, shovel-shaped head.

She looks over at Katrin again. Katrin's limbs are bent at funny angles to accommodate themselves to the shape of the footprint; she's almost quivering with the effort of holding the position.

"Look, Mommy, look Mommy, look!" Katrin calls, though Abby's looking right at her: Katrin in small, black Reeboks, purple stirrup pants, a purple headband. The pink sweater with white sheep on it that Katrin had picked herself from her drawer that morning. Her eyes that fix on Abby and don't look away, that forge into Abby surely and rightfully, as if she owned the place, as if she'd invented it.

Suddenly Katrin scrambles out. She comes running over in a burst of short footsteps. She's restless, Abby sees; they should go.

"Look, Katrin," Abby says, "look at the birds." Inside the case in front of them is a cast—a small rectangle of plaster embedded with bones, and framed in wood like a picture. *Archaeopteryx,* says the label, *the oldest known fossil bird.*

Abby watches Katrin's face, then realizes Katrin doesn't know what she's talking about.

"Is it chicken?" Katrin asks after a minute. It's true, Abby sees—the cast looks a little like the remains of dinner, the way the thin, delicate bones are strewn. Katrin turns away from the glass case, then she sighs and falls down on the floor next to Abby. Abby looks back at the fossil. There is something melancholy about the pale bones of the bird—something about the way they lie, flattened and splayed; the small skull turned sideways and bowed like a crucifix; the three featherprints etched among them like an aftermath.

Katrin is rolling on the floor with boredom. What is it, Abby wonders, that makes the bones hard to look at?

No limits in time and space—that's what I want with you. I have the image of us soaring, weightless, through the air.

Maybe it's imagining the terrible power of whatever had created this proof, the force that had surrounded this life and pressed it lastingly into the ground.

We are both so beautifully safe in all this.

Or maybe it's the randomness, she thinks, the way the bones are scattered, as if they'd been thrown down. They lie together, close but not touching, in roughly the shape and area a bird might have taken up, but nothing is in the right place.

You will always have me.

Her eyes search for order in the thin lines of bone, the wedges of white between them, the whispery impressions of the feathers. If she were a scientist, Abby thinks, she'd see it: the way the random pattern said something about the life of the thing, about the moment of its death.

You are beautiful and graceful and smart and alive.

What had she said back, Abby wonders. She can't remember. She'd lain in the dark, listening to his words like a child listening to a story, turning to marvel with him from the depths of his mind's eye.

You're the fantasy I would have had if I'd had the wit to invent you. I like saying these things to you—I'm amazed by my luck each time I do.

In the bathroom mirror at night, after she'd been with him, her eyes had never looked so dark to her, her mouth was a soft, black blur; she was all openings and no edges.

The idea of being together with you seems like the most brilliant thought ever constructed by the human brain.

Katrin gets up from the floor and takes off for the other side of the room again. Slowly, Abby moves to follow. She wants to keep looking at the bird.

"I have to get a life," Stephen had said at the end, sounding as if he'd discovered a new answer to a yes-or-no question.

"Because I have to get a life," he'd started to repeat, as if he were enjoying the sound of the words.

"Coming here to live—" he'd said, casting his eyes up briefly, like someone trying to remember what he'd been about to say. "I just can't picture it."

"What about your story?" she'd asked Stephen the last time he'd called, to tell her he wouldn't be coming back.

"What story?" he'd said.

"The one about your mother's house. Mortality. I was going to be in it. I suppose you can't write that now."

"No," he'd said, sounding resentful. "I can't write that now." Then after a minute he'd said, "Maybe I'll write a birthing story." To her silence on the other end, he'd added, "Everyone does."

Abby walks around the display of large vertebrates. Across the room, Katrin's standing with her head bent back, issuing sharp, barking shouts at the ceiling and listening for the echo.

There is something pleasing and still about the bones, even with Katrin's ruckus. Abby is standing behind the Indian Elephant, looking through the wide hole of its pelvis to the other side of the gallery.

She lets her focus shift lazily; she has the sudden thought, reflexively sad and then vanishing, that she would like to lie down on the floor of the mastadon's closing rib cage.

———

"*You* could write a birthing story," Stephen had said to her over the phone. He'd sounded skeptical. He changed the subject then, back to the reasons he was leaving, but she'd kept thinking about what he'd said. Maybe she could. She could write about how at the end, time seemed to fold itself in half like a laundered sheet stretched between two people, until there were just two moments: the one before—the unspeakable pain and the impossibility of what had to be borne, and then just the one—the irrevocable moment of terror and loss and beginning, as the thrashing ball of angry, helpless need expelled itself propulsively from her body.

Or, she thinks, remembering something, she could write about a dream she'd had. It was after Stephen had left, but before she'd known that he wasn't coming back. She dreamed they were traveling, without any clear sense of destination—just roaming around the desert. They'd found a restaurant, gone in, and sat down.

It was an ordinary place, except that underneath the tablecloth on Abby's side, so that only she could see it, the table was a wall of crumbling red sandstone, and something marvelous was happening: Abby was pulling out artifacts, unearthing beautiful objects one after the other—beaded leggings, silver bracelets, painted bowls.

She couldn't believe her luck. Each thing was whole and perfect, and the strange part of the dream was: They were hers. She'd found them, she wanted them, she was taking them greedily. Stephen had been watching her from across the table; she'd smiled up at him and handed him a tiny, carved wooden skull.

"I'll be over here, sweetie," Abby calls to Katrin, and she turns in the direction of the door.

"Love," Stephen had written to her on the back of a postcard, "like everything else on this planet, is subject to authorial revision."

"No it's not," she says. She stops, surprised, and listens to the words hanging in the empty air.

"Come on, Katrin," Abby calls again, and turns to see if Katrin's following her. As she does she sees something. There are dimensions, places, space blossoming from within the space in front of her. There, under the high canopy of the elephant's ribs, between its four tent-pole legs, is a small room. The cave bear's ribs look just like a basket.

The elephant's tail hangs in front of her face like a vine, visual flotsam; she turns her attention to it slowly. Slowly she lets her eye move down, not wanting to squander any of its painful, pleasing perfection.

What is the pain? Abby wonders. The pleasure, she thinks, is in the unexpected convergence of beauty and order: the way her eye eases over the long, graceful whole; the way the pieces snug together; the sight of the smooth, round chunks of white losing size in impossibly perfect decrements; order descending, bone by bone by bone. The pleasure is in the certainty that she's looking at perfection; it's in the way, she suddenly thinks, that perfection looks to her right at this moment: each small, essential thing held perfectly in place by the thing next to it; a lack of loss, nothing missing—nothing able to be.

"Katrin," she calls, "I'm going." She turns and moves slowly through the door, following the signs for the exit; she's surprised to see there's a whole room she hasn't been in. The Invertebrate Gallery. She realizes they've done it backward—missed the beginning of the exhibit.

She hears Katrin behind her, but doesn't turn around; she is moving through the room slowly, gliding past the rows of freestanding display cases, taking in the sight of the odd, petrified things, the words that accompany them.

Raindrop prints. *Impressions made by a brief rain shower on semimoist sediment.*

Resting traces. *Fossil evidence left by an animal that temporarily interrupts its locomotion in search of rest or refuge.*

Insects in amber. *The perfect mold of a body, where an insect, trapped in the oozing resin of an ancient coniferous tree, dried away.*

———

Katrin staggers up behind Abby punchily and leans against her legs. "Look, Mom," she says. She is holding her fist close to her chest, clutching something.

"What is it, sweetie?" Abby says. Katrin holds her hand toward Abby, but she keeps her fist clenched protectively. Abby wonders what Katrin imagines—if she thinks that the precious thing inside will leap out and disappear if she opens her hand. Abby bends down and Katrin opens her fingers a little bit—she's holding one of her tub toys, a small, peg-shaped plastic figure.

"Oh," Abby says, "a baby"—Katrin's generic term. "Where did you find it?"

"It's not a baby," says Katrin. "This is the princess. She was in my pocket."

"Oh," Abby says, "I thought they were all babies."

"No," says Katrin, as if she can barely suffer Abby's dimness. "Green baby's a baby and blue baby's a baby and the red one is the mother and she's a grown-up. And the white one with the yellow hat is a boy and he's nice, and this is the princess and she's sad."

Abby is astonished. All of the plastic people look alike to her. "Why is the princess sad?" she asks.

"See?" says Katrin, cheerily, matter-of-factly. She pushes the doll closer to Abby and points to its face, to show her how the doll's painted mouth turns down, clearly and cleanly, in an upside-down U. Then she smiles teasingly at Abby and takes off, running in that manic, shoulder-hunched way that Abby recognizes from childhood—the self-induced creeps. Giddiness turning to unease turning to terror; Abby smiles as she remembers the deliciousness of the fear. The instinctive childish pairing of the terror with its relief: the hall light, the warm bed, the familiar body coming back into view from around the thicket of bones.

FIVE DREAMS OF FALLING

She wakes up in Jasper's bed. Jasper's in the kitchen. Everyone she knows in this city has the same kitchen landscape, is her second thought on waking. Electric coffee grinder and empty refrigerator. Her first thought is of Jasper's face. She hasn't seen it in the light yet; she was sleeping when he came in last night. She'd taken a shuttle from the airport and let herself in with a key he'd left with his downstairs neighbor.

He'd woken her by standing over her.

"Hey," he said when she opened her eyes. She hadn't remembered what he looked like—he'd gotten both his ears pierced; his eyes were blue, not brown. He wore a necklace—something tribal looking, a hammered metal shape on a leather cord. On the wall above his desk was a photograph of a pretty woman wearing the same kind of necklace.

She twists in the sheets and stretches her body across the bed, leans her head out the open window. Outside, the bright sunlight burns onto the surfaces of things.

Three years before, she'd lain in Stephen's bed, across the city. "You have to be with me," he'd said. The same sunlight had been burning in.

She draws in her head and sits up. Jasper is handing her a cup of coffee and smiling. She studies him. She imagines the exact shape of the space that would be left if he suddenly disappeared.

Three thousand miles away, Abby has a five-year-old daughter, whom she's left with her someday-to-be-ex-husband for a year, to come live in this city and go to a school where she will learn how to spin sugar, paint with chocolate, conjure tiny animals out of marzipan. This is not a dream, though every morning she wakes up sweating, thinking of her daughter Katrin, wondering how much damage she is about to do.

Last night Jasper had held her face and said her name, and it had sounded odd to her—unfamiliar and then frightening. But then he'd pulled her gently onto him, and he stopped saying her name and started calling her baby, and she'd felt herself falling, not like in a dream, heavily downward, but away. Up into the dark corner of the room, where she hovered above the low music that was playing: blues, voice after voice moaning baby this, baby that. Up above the sound of Jasper's voice, and the red glow of the Christmas lights strung over the bed, to where she could see everything: She could see herself, falling over and over into Jasper, and Jasper hurting her—pulling her hair, a little too hard, because she's told him to, because it's been three years since Stephen left and she still can't feel anything.

She could see her suitcase, tucked neatly behind the bedroom door, and the picture of the girlfriend on the wall. She could see that Jasper would smile at her the next morning over coffee, and invite her to stay but hope she wouldn't; that she would wait until he left and then put her things together; that she would call her friend Sarah, and take his extra key, though she knew she wouldn't use it, and that she would leave something unasked for in return—her thin gold earrings, perhaps, the last gift her father had given her, or her favorite silver bracelet, that she'd bought when Stephen left; and that Jasper will never quite get around to getting them back to her, though she'll call every once in a while and get his machine; and that, stripped of these small, secret powers, though she'll lie in bed at night trying to summon his face, his voice, the unseen solidness beneath her, in the moments before drifting away from herself and off toward the frightening, inviting edges of consciousness, she won't be able to; she won't even be able to dream any of it.

Before Katrin, Abby had wanted children—lots of them. She'd wanted to go to the playground, the zoo, the wading pool; she wanted to sit on the floor and make things with origami paper and Plasticine, draw pictures with bright markers from flat tin boxes, play Candy Land, bake jam tarts and Christmas cookies and pigs in blankets.

That was before things had started to go badly, before she'd realized it was going to be a long time before colicky Katrin started to take an interest in arts and crafts, before they'd moved to a town without a playground and her someday-to-be-ex-husband had discovered he didn't want to "do the marriage thing," before she'd fallen in love with Stephen and he had left and she had cried every day for a year and a half, hoping each day for another day of grace— that Katrin would still be too young to remember any of it.

She had wanted three children. Girls, like the start of a fairy tale.

"I'm going to miss you, Mom," Katrin had said at the airport, the day Abby left. Katrin and her father were flying, too, to Minneapolis to visit his parents.

"I'll miss you, too," Abby had said, and something had happened that Abby couldn't forgive herself for. As she'd said it, she'd imagined something—she'd imagined Katrin's plane falling out of the sky, and the first thing she'd felt hadn't been the irreparable crack of grief, like she had ten years earlier, when her mother had hung up the phone and turned to Abby and said, "Dad's dead." Not even like when Stephen had called to tell her that he wasn't coming back, and she'd known in that moment that he was the one thing in the world she wouldn't be able to live without.

Her first thought, instead, had been a terrible, shameful one; she'd imagined her life, just for a moment, smooth and empty, like a big white dinner plate with nothing on it, and she'd felt herself turn, inwardly, to take a closer look at the thought.

She calls a cab to take her to Sarah's. Jasper had leaned to kiss her when he left; they'd both laughed at the awkwardness. Secretly, she'd been appalled: The small act had made her happy.

At Sarah's, there's a note telling her where the towels are, and to help herself to anything she finds, and directions to the nearest café. She finds Sarah's coffee grinder and beans, but no coffeepot; she dresses, in clothes of Sarah's, and leaves the apartment. She's forgotten what it's like to be in a city with good weather, the world divided into sunlight and shadow.

In her suitcase is a card, ten years old, with a picture

on it of a woman's head silhouetted in white space. The woman stares straight ahead, an entranced expression on her face. Through the whiteness, a butterfly flies toward her, carrying a dangling jewel.

She'd found the card when she was going through boxes, getting ready to leave. "Dear Abby," it read, "This is a lovely city. I am having coffee and looking across the bay at the hills. Love, Dad." It was the last thing he'd sent her.

As she leaves Sarah's building, she sees there's some kind of commotion up the block. A small crowd of people are standing on the sidewalk in front of the motel on the corner. As she gets closer, Abby sees that the people are gathered around a man who is sitting on the ground, leaning against the beige stucco wall of the motel, his legs covered with a blanket. An ambulance turns the corner and stops. Abby can tell from the way the people are moving around him that the man is all right.

It's only later, when she's waiting at the counter to order her coffee, that she thinks, maybe the man fell. And a moment later than that, as she exits the café into the bright sunlight, that she thinks: or jumped.

The last man she'd gone out with, in Massachusetts, had sat across from her at a restaurant and said, "I'm not one hundred percent satisfied and I don't know if it's fair to you to continue." There'd been a travel poster on the wall of the restaurant, and he'd kept looking at it.

"I wonder how the women are in New Zealand," he'd said to no one in particular, handing the waiter his salad plate.

He'd shown her a picture, that he'd taken on a trip out West, of a canyon—he didn't remember where. A paved two-lane road in the foreground disappeared between two massive canyon walls; in the distance, an indistinct valley—city or desert or farmland—whitened upward, evaporated into the sky.

She'd held the picture a long time. It could have been the place she grew up. She thought about being in a car with her father and her brother, descending from a day of skiing or a hike or a drive, the late afternoon light pink on granite, blue on snow. A song came into her head, something she didn't remember the name of; she thought of the way her father used to sing to the radio, delivering the words a second after he heard them, trying to match the feeling of the singer. "I like this picture," she said.

"I'm going to send it to my friend Larry," the man replied, taking the picture from her, sounding like someone who'd just quelled a laughing fit. "I think it looks like a big vagina. Don't you?" he'd said, pushing it closer to her face, but she'd blurred her eyes and looked away, and she hadn't told him what she'd been about to tell him, a secret she'd discovered one night when she was going through her father's slides: that if you looked at a canyon upside down, gravity would disappear in an exhilarating rush—road, river, or canyon floor would become a thick, palpable ceiling where you could hover, as tilted rock walls zoomed past you, inviting you to fall through them, and the sky opened beneath you like a world made of space and air and emptiness; like possibility, the absence of loss, no memory.

The crowd is gone when Abby passes the motel on the way back. She slows to look, from the other side of the street. Is there something on the sidewalk? She notices an odd smudge trailing down the stucco wall, from one of the second-story windows to the ground where the man had been.

Smudge isn't right. It isn't even a mark, exactly—it's more like a sheen, a wide swath of brightness, like the trail of a jet taking off. She can't imagine how the man could've made such a mark, then she realizes someone must have washed the wall—gotten up on a ladder and scrubbed whatever it was—blood, skin, threads from his clothing—that the man left on his way down.

The window is only two stories, twenty feet at most, above the ground. Why would he jump? Abby wonders. Or fall. Drunkenness, stupidity, miscalculation? Desperation? Or its opposite: some willful disbelief in the inexorability of gravity?

She thinks about Jasper. His apartment, in the dark, had been close and thrilling. She'd sat alone in the red glow, leaning up against a dark, mirrored Indian cloth wall hanging, watching the way the Mexican tin ornaments that hung from the moldings threw glints of red when she moved her head.

She'd imagined Jasper coming in the door, hugging her hello, getting a beer, sitting down to talk to her in the darkness. She'd imagined the muscles in her face relaxing, her heart unclenching.

She'd been trying to remember what he looked like. She'd wondered, almost randomly, if and when she would forget what Stephen looked like. She couldn't picture her father anymore, she thought with a sudden fear.

She crosses the street toward the motel. The smudge is gone, invisible from this angle; she looks at the blank, tan stucco wall. The words "bad end" are floating around in her head.

But the man who fell or jumped hasn't come to any end, she reminds herself. Maybe it was just some crazy thing—a story to tell his grandchildren one day. It was something you'd think you could only dream, he'd tell them, but this really happened: He was visiting San Francisco, staying in a motel on Van Ness—a little seedy, but the only thing he could find. It was a beautiful day, all sunlight and shadow, and he'd gone to sit on the sill, to take in the sight of the welcoming city and decide what to do next.

When what? She tries to think of a story her daughter would like, her daughter who is just at the edge of still believing in magical things.

"Are there any children in it?" Katrin would ask; Katrin would want there to be children.

A man has appeared from the motel's entrance. He is walking toward Abby.

When she gets back to Sarah's, she'll call Jasper and leave a message. Such pictures she's having, like waking dreams: Jasper saying her name, holding on to her in the darkness—two hands she doesn't even see, pulling her out of one place and into another. She pulls back; it feels to her as if they could extract each other from dark space, as if she could wring the darkness into life with her bare hands.

She puts her body to Jasper's, feels her power over him. She imagines her life. All the beautiful things she will soon be able to make: towering wedding cakes, quivering half-moon custards inside extravagant domed cages of burnt sugar, chocolate butterflies.

The man approaches with purpose. Abby imagines for an instant that he is going to say something to her, but he looks away. She drifts toward the curb and steps out into the street. When she is across, she turns to look; it strikes her as the oddest thing. He has a metal tape measure, and he's extending it up the smudged wall to the bottom of the window. Why? she wants to cross back and ask him. What will it tell him, to know exactly how far the man fell?

CLIFF DWELLER

I am not confused. I was the eighth of eleven children. My sister Evie used to dress the cat in doll clothes when the rest of us were gone to school.

The first time I saw it, I thought the world had merely flip-flopped to reveal the magic I knew lay on the other side of every day. I believed in God, Jesus, the Holy Ghost, fairies, hobgoblins, trolls, princesses, dryads, magic beans, so when the cat came slipping through the fence in a blue gingham blouse and tiny leghorn with a stem of wooden cherries on the brim, I was only surprised for a minute. I was angry when Evie ran through the gate a moment later, calling, and the world flopped right-side-up again, and I knew everything would be the same as always: chores, schoolwork, the dark bruise of my mother's eyes as she met us at the kitchen door.

"Are you confused, Baba?" Sarah says. I see her send her mother a look—form a question with her eyebrows—across the room. Sarah lays her hand on the shoulder of Abby's man friend. "This is Stephen. *Stephen.*"

I am not confused. I grew up in central Illinois. My father worked in the mines. My sister Evie used to dress the cat in doll clothes when the rest of us were gone to school. The girl, Abby, had a different man the last time I saw her—the father of the child, whom I can see out the window, playing in the yard with Samuel's youngest. A little girl, whose name I can't remember no matter how many times they tell me, because it's an odd name, like all the children's names nowadays, something slippery and smooth like lake water, just as easy to grab hold of. I was the eighth of eleven children. We were: George, Donald, Edward, Louise, Margaret, Dorothy, Bernard, Mary, William, Joseph, Evelyn.

"Pleased to meet you, Mary," says the man, Stephen.

"Your brother?" I ask Abby.

"No, Baba," says Sarah. She gives her mother the worried look again.

"No, Mama," says Mimi. "Not Jimmy. *Stephen.*"

"Your brother?" I want to hear her say what he is.

"My *partner*," Abby says. Like someone you choose for a dance.

Mimi took me to see Evie, but she was an old woman with yellow skin, lying in a rumpled bed. She wouldn't look at me. Her eyes stared somewhere else, as if she were that little child again, all the brothers and sisters gone.

Evie was the one I told; she was always my confidante. Even though we were too old by then, I led her out back to the winter-bare garden, crept with her into the hollow under the leafless wisteria, where she used to sit with the cat pinned and squirming in her lap, trying to feed it leaf tea from a tiny clay cup.

"What will you do?" she asked.

I barely knew him. He saw me at church and came to our door not long afterward; he took me down to the pond to skate. Where were my brothers and sisters that day? When we got there he put his cold mouth on my warm one, his cold fingers to my warm skin. He pulled me down onto the cold ground. I was confused; I didn't know what it was, then, that coldness trying to enter me, trying to find a home.

We walked in the graveyard a month later; we agreed to marry. We decided on names: Peter for a boy, Miriam for a girl. Back then you didn't know which it would be, like they do now.

He wouldn't stop reading the gravestones, and I tried not to listen. I was looking for the babies' graves. That's what my sisters and I did when we walked there together, each of us trying to be the one to discover the saddest thing.

"This one lived just three months"; "This one lived just a week"; "This one died the day it was born," as if by naming the sadness you didn't know, you could inoculate against it, quell the fear without looking it in the eye. But of course we didn't think of it that way, then, as we scampered from stone to stone, collecting the babies' brief lives like dropping berries in a bucket.

"Verlene and Edward Binns," he called to me from across the rows of stones. I remember those names, after all these years—two people who were dead then, deader now.

"Married forty years," he said. "This will be us, someday." TOGETHER IN ETERNITY, their stone read. Etched on it was a pair of linked hands. I would have made the hands separate, I remember thinking—reaching for each other—the space between them hanging like a choice, into eternity.

I told Evie I was convinced the child would be born dead. Cold, blue, made from the ice of that day—how could anything good come from the terrible thing I'd done? But I was wrong. Miriam was perfect, so were Peter and Sylvia and Samuel, too—each time, somehow, the ugliness of my life gathered into a terrifying knot and turned itself inside out like a shirt, sloughing another sweet and perfect being into the world.

The girl, Abby, smiles at me as if we have a secret. And I suppose we do: I know what she will tell us soon. I can tell by the way she rests one hand on her flat belly and reaches up with the other to hook the man's finger, leans back against him where he perches on the arm of her chair, casting a shadow across her like a four-o'clock sunset.

He never guessed, not once. It was only after I told him that he knew—he knew something else besides him was in me, then he'd come after me. Wherever I was, day or night: standing at the sink doing the dishes or upstairs ironing, folding work shirts and school blouses and creepers and little socks; he'd pull at my buttons, fold his arms across my neck, push his knees into the backs of my knees.

"So, Mary," says the man, Stephen. Leaning toward me, smiling like a wolf.

He thinks I don't know he knows: that another man has desired me more than anything else in a single moment. Pulled me down and mounted me like an animal. He thinks I can't see him imagining how it must have been. Wondering if I moved toward that dark place, too, or if I held still in fear, wishing to be anywhere but where I was, only temporarily safe from his random, exploding anger.

————

He would rage like the thunderstorms that gathered and broke at the end of every day in the late summer in central Illinois.

"All I want is a happy life!" he'd shout. I might be pulling myself up off the floor, rubbing my hip; I might be trying not to bleed on my blouse.

"I'm miserable!" he would bellow. "It's your fault!"

I'd find myself wishing for Evie, the garden, the fairies, the cat. If only I could make myself disappear, I remember thinking, maybe he won't wake the children.

But there was no magic, none of that sort, anyway. There was something else, something that enraged him: Every morning I would wake up curled into the warm cove of his sleeping body, his hand hanging heavy over my hip, and in that moment before I'd unmold myself from him and slide out of bed, I'd lie still and I'd feel the inexplicable miracle of my own forgiveness, smell it in the musk of our bodies that drifted up from under the quilt—the scent of something animal, yet wholly human, breathing, ripening, getting ready to spill.

He didn't want it, though.

"I love you," he'd say in the night, after the storm had spent itself. He'd burrow his face into my neck, push his hands up under my gown. In the morning, though, he'd be angry again. I never knew what happened to him between the night and the day; maybe he breathed in the fear and anger and injury that rose off me as I dreamed.

"Would you like more oatmeal?" I would ask the children. I was a smooth stone, I was a plant, breathing poison, exhaling pure, clean oxygen. I could feel his glare on the side of my face, though what he was looking for, I never understood, not in our whole life together.

"Shall I butter your bread?" And when I was finished with them, I would turn to him. "What would you like?" I would ask. That's how I started every day, until the one he didn't wake up. And surprised me: I always thought he'd go out raging. But he just turned toward the wall in the night, and when I opened my eyes in the blue light of the morning, he wasn't looking his question at me—his request for the daily offering he believed he required: the gift of myself, offered up like a china cup to an orangutan.

"So, how'd you wind up here, Mary?" Stephen asks.

We drove. He decided he didn't want to work in the mines. That was all right with me; I didn't have much of a soft spot for Illinois, though of course it wasn't easy leaving my brothers and sisters and my mother, the small country of my family waving us down the drive.

We went to the desert first. I was five months along with Mimi. The air was searing and dry as we climbed the long, hot path to view the Indian ruins, and I wasn't as beautiful to him, I knew, as when we walked in the cool, moist graveyard. From the moment we'd left central Illinois, I could feel his glare trying to penetrate my skin, like a worm boring core-ward, looking for a place to hide from the light of the widening landscape.

"I'm hot," he said, his voice a petulant child's.

"Well, sit down in the shade," I told him over my shoulder, but I didn't stop walking. A canyon had risen around us. I couldn't take my eyes off the place where the rock met the sky. Each new configuration was, I was sure, the most beautiful thing I'd ever seen in my life, until suddenly I crested a rise in the trail and the sight of a pink-orange cliff filled my eyes. First, all I saw was the wall of rock, thrown up where the horizon should be: vast and empty, like the end of the world; rosy, rock-solid oblivion.

Then the dwellings appeared. Burrowed in under the overhanging cliff, a warren of pathways and rooms and openings, stone and sun and shadow, someone's home.

As I continued toward the ruins, I imagined the lives gone from there. Mimi, inside of me, had started to make her presence known just a few days earlier; I remember the whispering feeling, as I walked, like someone painting me from the inside with a soft, small brush.

I saw children playing in the dirt; I could hear their shouts, and the murmuring voices of women: someone the world would never even imagine had existed, preparing food, pouring water from a vessel, tightening a strap, smoothing a child's hair. But when I turned to tell him what wonders were right there in front of my eyes, I saw his face was glowing, his mouth working in rage.

"How dare you talk to me like that?" he demanded. It was the first time he'd spoken to me in such a way, and it was as strange as if that cat, slinking past in its finery, had stopped to ask the way to town.

I turned again toward the ruins, empty now, the pictures chased out of my head. Where were the people I'd seen? Gone—I knew the difference between fancy and fact. I was the eighth of eleven children. My father worked in the mines in central Illinois, and every night when he came home, he'd cast an exhausted, black-tinged look over us all and disappear into the bedroom until my mother went in to fetch him for supper. I knew the difference between something that vanished completely and something that breathed, darkly, in the back of the house, gathering the strength to conjure itself to life again.

When I turned back to face him, he was nowhere in sight. The path we'd traveled flattened backward to empty desert. I was ashamed at how frightened I felt, standing alone in the ruins. I was the eighth of eleven children. I had never been alone in my life.

Everything will be all right, I remember I said out loud, and I felt the lie, like the windblown seed of an unfamiliar plant, sift down through the air and take root inside of me.

———

My children were perfect because I lied so well. I looked straight into the face of the ugliness and devoured it, took it into my own body, big mouthfuls of poison. I made my surface flat and smooth as desert stone.

This girl Abby will never be able to do it. I can see, just by looking at her. I can see the way she leans toward the man's voice like a plant toward the light. Her face is full of spaces and depths, shadows, furrows, secrets. She won't lie. She will wear the pain and the insults and the bruises there.

"Mary," Abby says, and she gets up from her chair and comes to sit next to me on the sofa. "Tell me how you are."

Choices, she and Sarah call the collection of odds and ends that make up their lives. They use the word all the time. Sarah learned it from her mother, no doubt, but where Mimi learned it has always been a mystery to me.

"Did you *love* him?" Mimi asked me once.

"At first," I said. She waited for more, but there wasn't. For a short time I did love him, but it hardly matters now, and in fact, it hardly mattered then—love the way Mimi meant it, like a story you tell with yourself at the center; a small, perfect house you build on top of a beautiful, far-off ridge.

"Don't you feel well, Baba?" Sarah asks. I wonder if she's guessed.

Mimi's eyes sharpen; her head turns. She guessed right away, almost as soon as I knew myself. Her sharp eyes wandered down my body one day when I was resting—chest, belly, face, all the places it shows.

There has always been something I liked about this time. Despite the tiredness, the sickness: I always felt as if I were inhabiting an odd interval of grace, a suspended moment that doesn't exist—the state of being entirely alone, which you only notice at the instant it stops being true, when the physical tribulation: The swelling, the tenderness, the wobbliness inside, edges into consciousness and announces who you *aren't*, suddenly, anymore.

"I'm taking you to the doctor on Monday," Mimi says.

It isn't necessary, I told her before. I've done this alone so many times.

They take pictures, now, wire you to machines, tell you things you already know, things you don't need to know: how big or how small it is, how long it's been growing, whether or not it will be perfect.

"But I'm concerned," she said, and I knew I would let her. Because isn't that my job? To take away their fears? To keep them warm and fed and safe from the things that can hurt them? Creep out of the room, slowly, after they're asleep, close their door and go out, alone, to face him, to agree to whatever it was he said I'd done that day so he would eventually quiet—stop shouting, pounding the walls, rattling keys, scraping chairs out of the way to get to me.

"If you don't shut up, I'll make you sorry," he'd threaten. "If you speak to me like that again, I'll break everything in this house," and he would: chairs, dishes, mirrors, the children's toys, the telephone.

He closed my mouth. He did. I saw that's what he believed he'd been put on God's green earth to do, and I let
him. He might have killed me otherwise, and the children
needed me; in the beginning, it was as simple as that.

What I came to tell Evie, that day I found an old woman
lying in her skin, was: I'm afraid our days of grace are over.
This one isn't perfect. I don't know how I know.

I made a mistake. I thought we were finally safe. The
children had been gone so long; I'd hiked them over the
high mountain of their childhood, felt myself becoming
weightless as I watched them descend, gathering speed,
down the other side. Some nights, waiting for sleep, I would
get a strange, calm feeling, like being carried out of my
own life on the cloud of forgiveness that billowed past, dis-
sipating into the wide, white sky.

The night he died, for the first time in my life, I defied
him. Would it kill you to be nice to me? I asked, my voice
a crimson streak through black air. To my surprise, he didn't
jump up. Probably he was too tired to fight. His hand came
slowly toward me in the dark.

They want to perform tests, cut it out of me, poison it.

It's different for these girls. If something's not perfect,
they hold it away from themselves with two fingers, turn
their noses up like petulant storybook princesses. I've heard
about the teenagers who throw babies in the garbage, flush
them down toilets.

I heard them talking in the kitchen this afternoon.

"I don't understand," Sarah said. The teapot whistled, and I heard water pouring into a mug. I pictured her holding it to her lips, closing her eyes, breathing in steam. "Why you wouldn't leave a man who did this to you."

I heard the rustle of newspaper. She likes to read the stories aloud, like my sisters and I, gamboling through the graveyard: men shaking babies, killing rivals, touching daughters, setting wives on fire.

"I would," she said, "in a minute," and I have no doubt.

"I *know*," said Abby, but she didn't sound as sure.

I hope her baby will be perfect. But they aren't all. Perfect beings, perfect lives, unwinding like a story you tell as you gaze out at evening falling over the distant valley from your little house on the ridge.

Then what? Do you turn away, contract your skin, let your insides dry and fall out like dust? Do you leave? Do you tell them to stay out, when they come to you, hurt babies, scared of monsters, scared of themselves, in the night?

Outward you open, and they come in; they are small, and you are large; you erase your edges and breathe out sweet air, fill yourself with the exhalations you've taught yourself to survive on.

"Wouldn't you think," Sarah said to Abby, "one day you'd decide you'd just had a bellyful? And leave? Simple as that?"

But who will love the ugly things? When they come to you and beg for forgiveness. On their knees, for God's sake, in the middle of the night? I was the only one on God's green earth who ever saw him, rocking back and forth in the dark, crying like a baby for what he'd done. I let his words dissolve into the air, I heard only the note. I could recognize each of my children's cries with my eyes closed.

Sometimes, if I tried hard, I could make the pale orange of a rock wall wash over the insides of my eyes. Listening to his words, as they lost their meaning, I'd picture him a disappearing cliff dweller crouched between the rocks, no trace of him left on the world except what existed in my eyes.

"No one has the right to wreck someone else's life," said Abby bravely.

"You're right," said Sarah. "No one does."

"What will you do?" Evie asked under the wisteria that day. If she could, she'd ask it now. The answer is the same.

Maybe the one inside me now is a monster, extra fingers and toes, misshapen head, heart's chambers jumbled. Maybe it will come out gnashing and clawing, trying to kill me, like that cat. My sister Evie used to dress the poor thing in doll clothes when the rest of us were gone to school. When I saw it walk by, I tried to pick it up, but it twisted in my arms, dug two sharp claws into my chest and sprang away.

Evie knelt to drag the cat from where it crouched, cursing us, under the bushes. She clutched it between her knees, began threading its thrashing legs into little eyelet knickers.

"Poor thing," she said, and for a minute I thought she was talking to me—my chest, where I rubbed it, still smarted. But she was looking down into the cat's grimacing face. She loved it, because no one else did, and in that way, it belonged to her.

BING-BING AND BONG-BONG

Condiments first—they're relatively few and easy, and no one cares, out there, what brand of mustard they spread on their sandwich, though inevitably someone will make the joke: Pardon me—as the rafts pass one another back and forth on the flat stretches where we'll drift for lunch if I'm sure nothing hairy's coming up—but do you have any Grey Poupon?

Also, the condiment aisle's right there near the line of carts if you walk in the northwest door of Safeway, though if you enter through the northeast door, you'll be in Produce, which I prefer to pick up last.

One large Dijon mustard. One low-sodium soy sauce. Canola oil, olive oil, olives for the puttanesca. Strictly California—the last time I used Kalamatas, four people picked them out: David Breen, the neurotic anesthesiologist from Denver, and his colorless brother, Don; Judith, who has her redeeming qualities, though appreciating fine cooking is not one of them; and Karen Garcia's friend, Doug Something, an able-bodied man who for some reason was unable to load and unload boats, and will not be invited again.

Five small mayos, one for each day, because they'll sit in the hot lunch bucket all day and it's always better to be safe than sorry.

It was easier when I had a different person plan lunch every day, but Kenneth put an end to that—Kenneth, who, the last time it was his turn, hiked the group a half-mile away from the river to the top of a scree-sided promontory to sit in the blistering noonday sun, and presented us with rock-hard mini baguettes, bought at great expense (ours) from a gourmet store in Phoenix, unpasteurized French cheese, and a reeking, bubbling jar of kimchi.

Kosher dills, ketchup, two squeeze margarines. Which will drive Stephen wild, but he's never (I never point out) the one who has to scrape sandy, hardened butter out of the bottom of the cooler after the trip is over. Or the one who has to bleach the coolers, untangle lines, sort straps, patch boats, haul equipment up the hill to the storage shed.

No, he's the one winging his way to the next place: the

next extended visit with friends, trip to Europe, project, woman.

"Home is where the house-sit is," I made the mistake of joking to him the last time he was on his way out. Maybe I was sick of crossing his name out of my address book, trying to figure out where to forward his mail, routed c/o me, fielding calls from women I'd never met: "Hi, is this Jamie? I was wondering, have you heard from Stephen?", varying degrees of curiosity and/or desperation in their voices; receiving the latest postcard with his current information on it. Where I could call him in case something really important happened. Our mother dying, for example.

Cereal—two puffed rice, one shredded wheat, three granolas, two instant oatmeal. Take the price tags off the granola so Stephen doesn't see. He'll mention the boneless chicken breast as it is and we'll be at it, no matter what I say: two forty-year-old brothers producing a feedback effect with each other's mild high blood pressure, and I suppose you could call it love. Only it doesn't feel like love, exactly. Comfort, maybe. Maybe even something less than that. Familiarity, recognition—like two last, lone animals of the same species running into each other on some wide and lonely plain, where, in truth, when we're not thinking about it, which is almost always, we are perfectly happy to be.

American food is the worst. Though United is only a speck less vile. I would gladly have done without the food,

and, incidentally, saved myself ninety-nine dollars, by flying Morris, but, of course, Jamie called with his plan a day
too late.

I suppose the ninety-nine dollars is money well spent,
because I'll be spending time with Jamie, something I'm always happy to do. Still, it would have been better if he'd
called a day earlier. Ninety-nine bucks is ninety-nine bucks.

I wasn't doing anything, anyway. Taking long walks, going to the library, clearing my head between projects.
Spending time with friends who haven't seen me in a
while. Looking at a rent increase of one-seventy-five a
month, thinking about getting out of San Francisco, moving to Seattle, Portland, L.A. Nothing pressing. Eight days
on the Green with Jamie sounded as good as anything.

Apparently this is chicken. Provençal? *À la chausseur?*
Helper? It doesn't matter—whatever it is, I'm going to eat
it. It cost me ninety-nine bucks, after all.

Twenty-four envelopes instant hot cocoa, two packages Earl
Grey, two Red Zinger, two Sleepytime, ten cans evaporated milk. Five pounds of coffee—you always need more
than you think, though I can cheat with the decaf (which
no one ever wants unless I forget to bring it) if we run out.
I don't mind being up then, before everyone else—before
the bleary, ravaged-looking coffee drinkers appear, hover-
ing like clumsy, cranky ghosts, hoping someone else will
have gotten there before them.

I like the sounds from that time of day: the absence of human voices, the echo of wrens off the canyon wall, the white noise of the river, rushing or roaring, depending on rate of flow, the full-blast roar of the two butane burners; I like being the one to hand people a cup, unfold them a chair, start the breakfast preparations, and if the coffee's weak, no one ever complains. No one, of course, except Kenneth, who, when he decides to run his own trip because no one else does it exactly right, brings his *"Bodum"* as he calls it, a goddamn glass coffeepot in the wilderness. Four cups' capacity for seven competitive coffee drinkers, which turns out to be academic, because, as I predict as soon as I see it, it breaks the first day.

"Shit," Kenneth said. "What are we going to do for coffee?" because, naturally, he had no contingency plan— no instant, no backup pot, no filters, only twelve-hundred dollars' worth of red snapper fillets, swordfish steaks, loin lamb chops, frozen shrimp, fresh scallops for ceviche, a precious net bag full of Israeli tomatoes, six tiny heads of hydroponic lettuce, a collection of little festering bundles of watercress, cilantro, savory and dill, and five pints of Häagen-Dazs on dry ice, which we ended up eating as soup for breakfast on day two.

"Look," he said, as he removed the loose pieces of glass, maneuvering the plunger past the jagged mouth. "We can still use it."

"Throw it away," I told him. He was right: I broke the

rules on that trip. The rules are, the trip leader is the one in charge, the one responsible for everyone's well-being at the end of the day. It was his job, not mine, to picture one of us, three days into the wilderness, sticking an arm into the dishwater and coming up with the broken coffeepot and a severed radial artery.

Stephen, of course, hates Kenneth, so I'll have to keep them separated, like rivalrous children.

It was the middle of the day, of course, when Jamie called. At full rates. He calls me compulsive, asks why I care. I don't mention the two thousand dollars he borrowed from me three years ago and hasn't said anything about since. I don't point out that in effect I'm the one paying for these phone calls to me in the middle of the day, the thirty-dollar bottles of wine he "treats" me to, the sun-dried tomatoes he puts in his soups and stews—*peasant* dishes, for Christ's sake—the mail-order birthday shirts I would always rather do without.

I'll go on this trip, but it gets harder every year. I'm going because my mother called and said, "Jamie sounds lonely," and asked if I'd talked to him, if he was all right, if everything was okay between him and Gerri.

No, of course I didn't say to her, everything's never been okay between Jamie and Gerri. Why am I the only one who sees it? The way he knocks himself out running their life, which she occasionally checks into when her schedule permits it. Running *her* life—Christ—the woman hasn't bought herself tampons in the last fifteen years.

He picked up the L.L. Bean catalog last time I visited. I had cooked a chicken, and we were sitting at the kitchen counter watching it shrivel through the glass door of the oven, waiting for Gerri. "Must be a tough consult," he said, watching me eye the chicken.

"What do you think?" he asked, leafing to a page in the catalog and pointing to a cream-colored blazer. "For Gerri," he explained, mistaking my fury for puzzlement. "Wouldn't this be nice for conferences?"

But I never say anything. Because this is the form our love takes. It's what I can do for him: take his teasing, accept his gifts, appear when he summons me, listen to his problems without comment, let him think he's taking care of me. Besides, my mother's old; she could die any day. If it makes her happy to think of Jamie and me on a trip together, I'm glad to do it.

Coffee filters, paper towels, toilet paper, Tampax—an item, incidentally, I'm never without, since the day I amazed a crying woman outside a gas station rest room near Tuba City by pulling one out of my backpack, where I always kept them, back in the days when Gerri had time to backpack.

A month ago I got a letter from our mother. Rather, it was an envelope, stuffed fat with miscellaneous items: coupons, an advertisement for a product called Beano, a crossword puzzle from the previous Sunday's *Times*, which I'd already done, and a long article—three annoyingly folded L-shaped segments with the headline missing, its subject, apparently, the growing scientific evidence that some people are just born miserable. If she'd meant to put a note in the envelope, she'd forgotten, but she'd highlighted a spot in the article: "Even as children, they are irritable, negative and hard to reach, often experience feelings of rage and persecution, and fail to respond to affection like other members of the same family." She'd put two exclamation points in the margin next to the highlighted sentence and written, "S?" Two days later she called to say she thought Stephen needed cheering up. Was there anything I could do?

Jamie's invited that prick, Kenneth, along. Unbelievable. Kenneth spends the whole time, every trip, trying to think up ways to get under Jamie's skin; it seems he's settled on risking other people's lives as the most efficacious method.

There's a story Jamie likes to tell that illustrates, perfectly, the difference between my brother and me. In Jamie's version, providence, or maybe it's life's comic irony, spares the two of us, there on the wide riverbank. We'd run down to the shore in a storm to untie the boats and row across to camp, when a bolt of lightning hit the tree where the bowlines were hitched, from which I'd just removed my hand.

"You should have *seen* the look on his face," Jamie says. And laughs, bugs out his eyes. Mimics me, glancing, chastened, toward some imaginary maker.

But in my version, which is the truth, none of us would have been out on the unprotected bank in the first place if it hadn't been for Kenneth, who'd disappeared from the group, as usual, and delayed our departure, which should have taken place when the sky turned unexpectedly dark. Jamie, instead of being pissed, was *concerned*. So while he put everyone in one of the boats and rowed them across to a more protected spot, I—because I knew if I didn't, Jamie would—went to look for Kenneth. And found him *meditating* on a goddamn rock, with his eyes closed, a quarter of a mile away.

That's the difference between my brother and me. I was nearly killed as a result of the actions of a fucking dipshit who consistently flouts the rules, and who, for some reason, Jamie persists in inviting on his trips, and Jamie turned the whole thing into a *schtick* to entertain his friends with. Sometimes he reminds me so much of our father.

Bread we'll get at The Grain Exchange. Three white, three wheat, two honey oat, two sunflower, two dill, two light rye, six sourdough baguettes, and a dozen cinnamon rolls. It's expensive, even with the 20 percent discount on orders over forty dollars, which they always forget to give you unless you ask, but no one seems to mind—not even, amazingly, Stephen. His miserliness is whimsical—he doesn't mind spending eighteen dollars a pound on imported cheese if he gets it in his head to do so, or large sums for fresh flowers, something I couldn't care less about, when he comes to visit, but he'll burn ten dollars' worth of gas to save three dollars on a pair of shoes; he upbraids me for buying out-of-season produce, anything mail-order; whole salmon, wild mushrooms, sun-dried tomatoes for entertaining friends, if he doesn't deem them, the intended consumers, worthy; he won't buy a chicken breast someone else has boned.

I never say anything, though. I learned long ago not to question when Stephen gets something in his head. Not to look for a reason, because *that*—having gotten it in his head—*is* the reason. Something lodged, irksome, inflammatory, like a splinter, at which point there's nothing to do but sit back and watch—stay out of the way, keep my mouth shut. Sometimes he reminds me so much of our father.

Maybe I should buy a house. I'm at the age where a person should have a house. Find a small one that needs fixing, ask Jamie to do the repairs. Pay him, of course. I know he'd be glad for some paying work. That's the kind of thing our mother means, I think, when she asks us to take care of each other.

Who knows what it'll need—a roof, clapboards, skylights. I've always wanted a skylight. Though being tall does have its advantages, I've never liked the feeling of the ceiling bearing down on my head.

I remember the year I got taller than my father. How happy it made me, how mad he was. I was only thirteen; I grew so much that year, it hurt. He started calling me names—Weed, Timber, Galoot—making fun of the way I looked in my clothes, telling me it didn't matter how big I got, he was still my father. I remember how it felt, the liberation in shooting past him, one day being able to just look over his head, the daily dose of his vitriolic blowhard poison wafting harmlessly around my chest.

Jamie, of course, never grew taller than Ralph, a fact he turned into something to be proud of, since he could never pass up a chance to compete with me.

Every time I come to visit, at some point, as if he's never done it before, he goes to the front closet and gets out our father's old work jacket, the one that says RALPH on the pocket. Turns it around and around, touches the fabric, says, "Remember this thing?" And tries to get me to put it on. Makes me go through the motions, proving again—I put one arm in and get stuck with a wrist sticking six inches out; I can't even reach the other armhole—how small a man Ralph really was.

"It's even small on me," Jamie says. Every time. Then he helps me off with the binding jacket and slips into it himself, and I never say, because of the way it feels to me that, for Jamie, much depends on the sameness—and the wrongness—of his rituals, his stories, "No it's not, Jamie. It fits you perfectly."

So there it is, a plan. I'll buy a little house. Someplace cheap, Portland, probably. Spend some time in Salt Lake first—not a place I particularly like—hang out with Jamie. There's always a lot I can help him with: shopping, cooking, hauling down equipment, keeping him from getting his time wasted by all the "friends" who start coming around, suddenly, when river running season starts.

He'll need me to make some things: the mole, which I always do; a couple of lunch salads. Shop for the produce, which I hope he won't buy before I get there—all that high-profile, out-of-season chichi crap he likes to impress his parasitic acquaintances with. If he leaves it to me, I'll get whatever's cheap: beets, cukes, carrots, beans, peppers. Marinate them. Poke around in the herb garden. I like beets in a marinated salad; if anyone has a problem with that, they can fuck themselves.

Bleach, dish soap, dish scrubber, lantern sleeves—small items it's easy to forget and, though you might not think it, extremely hard to do without. Items, also, that it's not worth sending someone else out for at the last minute—no one but me has ever been able to locate the lantern sleeves (aisle eight, in the back half of the seasonal items section, between water toys and fishing supplies, usually about four shelves up).

I remember the exact moment I understood that for Stephen, reasons were cold, hard facts mined like rocks from within himself and, as such, presented to the world absolute, unalterable, fully formed. We were kids, playing a game in our driveway in northeastern Vermont—one for which Stephen, of course, had made up all the rules. Stephen made up the rules to all our games—the elaborate, intense, now unreconstructable competitions that were the main pastime of our childhood.

We were banging a tennis ball against the side of the garage—no rackets, just our hands—and he was howling, "No! No! That's not the way it goes!" His distorted glower was fixed on something invisible in front of him, some large, dire, infuriating obstacle only he could see.

"Like *this*," he kept insisting, as if he were the keeper of the most complicated, crucial secret in the universe. The longer he demonstrated, though, the less aware of my presence he became, the more agitated. Muttering, cheering, yelling at himself—having fun, in his own peculiar way, which wasn't, honestly, all that different from now: every moment fraught with the possibility of blowup, meltdown, failure of external circumstances, despair.

Cheese, assorted. Two and a half pounds rock shrimp;

two and a half pounds imitation crabmeat, the latter of which will make Stephen happy and I'll ask him to make the seafood salad for Day Two lunch, into which he'll put dill and lemon thyme from the garden, and Indian spices, and the old beets from the vegetable drawer if I don't remember to throw them out.

The first night is always particularly excruciating. I can never tell: Does he just not see it, or does he do it deliberately—make himself ridiculous, and if so, what does it prove? That Jamie and I have a legacy after all, that our father left us something besides the genetic predisposition to drop dead in our late fifties: buffoon-hood?

When we walk through the supermarket, for example, I almost can't stand to be there. He stops at every department—fish, deli, florist; he calls each person by name. "This is my brother, Stephen," he tells them. "Stephen, this is my friend Bill." Who is not his friend at all, who probably loathes him.

"Hello!" our father would boom, to anyone and everyone—he could be right in the middle of humiliating me publicly, telling me I'd better get my thumb out of my ass, stop acting like a girl, adjust my goddamn attitude; dressing me down for missing an easy grounder at Little League practice, or wearing my hair long, or being a sourass because I didn't think his jokes, or the chiding, aggressive chitchat he bathed us in constantly, were funny or entertaining. But he could still turn to a stranger, invariably someone there to serve him in some way, smile broadly, and say, "Hello! Bill!", reading the name off the name tag.

Jamie insists people liked our father, and though he's wrong, I suppose it makes sense that he believes it. Because he was always right there: riding in the front seat, standing next to Ralph looking over his shoulder in the hardware store, the lumberyard, the auto parts store, the shop—too close to see the rolled eyes, the forced smiles, the gestures and looks of barest tolerance, and, toward us, pity, while I hung back and saw everything clearly, which has always been my particular, unfortunate gift.

Dinner the first night is key. There's always a moment, after cleanup—everyone's gotten quiet, sitting around the fire, full from the meal, tired from the sun, from rowing and un-loading boats, and there's a silence. Everyone is waiting for whatever it will be that sets the tone of what comes next—someone telling a joke, someone taking out a bottle, some-one getting up and saying, "I'm tired. I guess I'll turn in." These are the moments that set the fragile mechanism of the group in motion for the next five or six days, and it's the trip leader's job to help things along. Stephen's wrong when he says people resent my efforts—jealous, probably, that his presence in a group has the effect of Godzilla walk-ing down Main Street, scattering the villagers.

———

It's inevitable—right after dinner, he starts doing his thing.

"Okay," Jamie says, breaking the after-dinner peace, "I have a couple things to show you." Then he looks at me and raises his eyebrows, and I have no choice. Or rather, my choice is, I can be the one to embarrass him, by pretending not to know what he wants and making the game fall flat, or I can participate and help him embarrass himself.

Can he really not see how unfunny it is? How the whole thing—the gesticulating; the dramatic pauses; the absence of any instruction, except that you just have to go along with the unpleasant thing happening to you; and the object—to make innocent people players in their own humiliation, for the entertainment of others—replicates our father's idea of sport exactly?

"Come here," Ralph would say.

If you asked, "What for?" he'd repeat, "Just come here." Next would come a question to which there were only wrong answers, including yes and no.

"You know what this is?" he might ask, holding up an object. The trick was that the object was never what it was—a drill bit left out of its case, or a screwdriver or a bicycle or an extension cord or a glass of water—it was an actual, physical emblem of your stupidity, not to mention your intent to harm him, the thing that was going to trip him on the way down the stairs and send him to the hospital; or put out his eye; or puncture one of his new radials when he drove over it in the driveway; or stain the dining room table he'd refinished himself.

Or he might ask you to perform an action: "Would you like to show me the proper way to close a door?" If you answered honestly, "No," and started on your way to do something else, you'd catch a hand across the back of the head, a fist between the shoulder blades.

"You know what this is?" Jamie says to me, holding up an imaginary object.

He's gotten everyone to gather around in a circle. I sit to his left or right, a look of mock bemusement on my face. I raise my eyebrows, shake my head, an idiot mime. No. I don't know what it is.

"This is the bing-bing," he tells me. To which I must respond, tilting my head with feigned fascination, "The what?"

He: "The bing-bing."

Me: "Ah, the *bing*-bing!" I take the imaginary object from him, examine it, then turn my head, owl-like, to the person on the other side of me, hand him or her the object, and say, "This is the bing-bing," while Jamie turns to the person on his other side, produces a second imaginary object, and says, "*This* is the bong-bong."

Then we wait, listening to the babel that ensues, while Jamie sits, smiling, surveying, like the patriarch of some big, silly family. The game ends when one hapless person gets the bing-bing from one direction and the bong-bong from the other and all the talking suddenly ceases, and that person either dissolves into laughter, or, just as likely—why can't Jamie *see* this?—becomes profoundly abashed, the two stupid objects dead-ended in his or her outstretched hands.

I've never reminded Jamie of the epic games he and I used to invent, using whatever we had on hand: a ball, a rock, a jackknife, a stick—nothing like this inane circle, with its absence of rules, and the losing built in. Our games were *about* their rules—elaborate ones we'd spend days, weeks, sometimes the whole lifetime of the game inventing and refining. It was the high point of our childhood, as far as I'm concerned, but Jamie seems to have forgotten. Another thing Jamie seems to have forgotten: We would never, ever have invented a game in which there was no clear winner.

The difference between us is this: I can pack a box and Stephen can't, and he'll hold that fact against me for the rest of my life.

When I pack the kitchen box I can feel his disapproving glower irradiating my back, and I always tell him if he can think of a better way, to feel free. Even though I know it's a no-win situation: He watches me pack it and gets mad, or he tries to pack it himself and gets mad. If it were his trip, he tells me every time, he'd bring two kitchen boxes. But it's not his trip, I never point out, and I also never point out that I have no problem packing the box. As a matter of fact, I *like* to do it. It's my *thing*, I'd say to him, if I didn't know it would make him mad to hear. To be presented with a few cubic feet of space and a jumble of objects—sharp, fragile, awkwardly configured—and to be able to fit them inside so that the lid closes without forcing.

It's a question of looking—another thing I can't tell him, because it's always been a talent of mine he doesn't share: You look for a minute at the limits of the space to be filled, the items you have to work with, and then—this is the hard part—you don't look again. You just get the shape of the emptiness in your head, or in whatever part of you knows shapes, space, possibility and its lack: the language of the limits of things—and you let the pile tell you what to do with it.

"It's like geometry," I want to tell him, but of course I don't. He was the smartest kid in the school, a year younger than me. We parted ways in junior high school geometry, though.

He claims not to remember his nights of raging. He'd stare at the book, muttering axioms and corollaries to himself, looking from it to me, as if what was in there proved, somehow, my traitorousness.

"What are you *saying*?" he'd end up screaming at me,

his voice reverting to the shrill tones of childhood, and I wouldn't answer: It was what I was *seeing*—pictures, of lines, planes, angles falling together to form perfect figures in space, which somehow bypassed his brain.

Sometimes, after I'd finished my homework and left it where Stephen could see it, I'd take my graph paper and pencils and go down to our father's workshop. I'd look at whatever he was making, touch it, admire it, ask if I could help with the finish work if I was careful.

It's no mystery, I want to tell Stephen, every time he goes to pack the kitchen box—the things came out of there; they can be made to go back in. Only not by the force of his will, the mere fact of his wanting them to. He'll have to do it my way. Which he won't. Because he can't give it up—the banging and cursing and remonstrating, his yearly reproach for my having left him behind all those years ago, for having a facility with pencils and shapes and tools and wood, for drawing shapes he couldn't see out of the random monotony of the tiny squares, for not joining him in his ongoing despair, for not hating our father.

Jamie and his fucking kitchen box. His fucking life lessons, his fucking *routines*. Everything has to *stand* for something; nothing can ever just be the bite in the ass it really is. Yes, I've never said to him—they came out of there, so of *course* it's possible to put them back in. But if it pisses you off to try, why not just bring a different box?

One case Coke, one case Sprite, one case Diet 7UP, three cases Spritzers, assorted flavors. Two cases club soda, one case iced tea, four cases Tecate, two cases Natural Lite. Eight beverages per day per person, plus an extra two cases. It's the one thing you can't risk running out of, though, of course, I could keep us alive, filtering river water like I had to on the trip when Kenneth tried to kill us every way he could think of. He'd taken all our pooled money and spent it on three hundred cans of Fosters. No juice. No soda. One five-gallon container of water that was gone the second day.

That trip was when I vowed I'd never go on another one with either Kenneth or Stephen again, but here I am. Remembering what I know: that every human emotion transforms itself into some combination of disappointment, obligation, and resignation in the end.

Day Four was particularly bad. Three hours for breakfast, while the sun rose high in the sky. We should have been six miles down the river, stopped for lunch in the shade, but instead, we were waiting for Kenneth's new portable stove to cool down enough to be able to pack it. We had corn bread for breakfast, though—one tiny square each.

"Arrivederci," Kenneth called, as he climbed into his kayak and pushed off the shore. He played cat and mouse with the boats all day, while I tried to keep track of whether he was

in front of us or behind, and watched the sun, and wondered where, since he was the captain, he would choose to camp. Not his favorite spot, I hoped, the mouth of a picturesque side canyon, where, I knew, I would stay awake all night worrying about the fact that if it stormed in the night, ninety miles away, a wall of water and debris would come rushing down the canyon and kill us.

That's where he was waiting, though. We turned the bend, and Kenneth leaped off the bank, kayak and all, and into the water in front of us, scaring the living shit out of everybody.

"Boo!" he chortled. "Beautiful spot, no?" He paddled back up onto the sand, got out of his kayak, and scampered down the beach like a kid. Shadow had already crept all the way up the walls of the canyon; it was my job, apparently, to get the boats unloaded, to help everyone find a tent site out of the wind, set up the toilet and the kitchen and start cooking dinner before it turned completely dark. Kenneth, I could see, had climbed to a fifty-foot ledge a little way downriver, and was doing his own, absurd version of t'ai chi, too close to the edge.

I wasn't aware Stephen had come up behind me till he spoke.

"Prick," he muttered, looking over my shoulder at Kenneth, such hatred in his voice, then he turned and stalked off down the beach. I watched him start hoisting things off the boats, stepping between the others without acknowledgment, his brow lowered, his fists clenched, his tall frame as uncomfortable on the land as on the water or anywhere else. Stephen was so thrilled when he grew taller than the rest of us, but its main effect was to make him hunched and isolated, and not even in demand for basketball, because he was such a pill on the court.

I watched him drag his things all the way up the beach to an exposed rock ledge, where he'd never be able to stake his tent. I knew, with a familiarity that made me feel weary, that something was going to happen. It was Abby who walked into it. This was the day *before* she and Stephen fell in love, not that I couldn't see that disaster coming from two miles away. She came lugging her dry bag up the bank, past Stephen, and with a final effort heaved it onto the sand near a rock.

"That's the *kitchen*," Stephen said, his voice still full of the odd hatefulness. It wasn't the unprovoked nastiness, though, that made me realize my well of patience with Stephen had dried up almost completely; it was what came next—the utterly unforgiving, killed-off look in his eyes when Abby replied in a tone that could have come from Stephen himself: "Says who?", not knowing, of course, the size of what she had just said. She turned her back and walked away.

It was a moment I'd been living all my life—the killed-off look, like something washed away from the inside, something worn out from so many moments of disappointment, the loss of love—even the love of strangers—over and over again. And I knew where I had seen it: on my father. I thought it meant that Ralph knew something about the world was killing him, and I can see how hard I always worked to make sure it wasn't me.

What Jamie pretends not to understand is that his mother-hen routine is so absolutely unnecessary. He thinks his concern is purely generous; he thinks by the force of his will, we'll all get along. I don't know why he can't see it for what it is: egotism, plain and simple. The idea that what one does has the power, really, to affect or alter even a moment of someone else's life. You love people because you choose to. Not because you need them to plan your meals or buy your clothes or show you to the toilet or tell you where to put your goddamn tent.

Here's another thing Jamie remembers wrong. The night before our father's fatal heart attack, Ralph spent fighting with me. He couldn't go out without one last bout of his favorite pastime. Red in the face, spitting, the whole nine bits, as he once said to me—he always fractured phrases, but that one was a triple boner, because he thought he was making a golf metaphor at the time. He was yelling his favorite thing to yell at me, the thing I hated most: "Do what you want, you will, anyway," because I'd told him I was assuming a nom de plume. My career was going well, my novel was being published.

"I don't know why, Ralph," I'd said, infuriating him even more. "Do I really have to have a reason?"

"Don't fight with your father," our mother begged, looking stricken. But I did, and I killed him.

"It's not true," Jamie told me. "He had heart disease. He played eighteen holes of golf that morning in the ninety-degree heat. He had fifteen men threatening to walk out of the shop the next day.

"And," he added, "your fight wasn't even that bad."

Flour, sugar, brown sugar, honey for tea. I don't know why Stephen and Ralph hated each other so much. I never figured it out. And it's true they did; their enmity was something outsized, corporeal, like a monstrous child they'd spawned, and to which they were devoted. Frankly, it was tiresome, the same way it is to be around any egregiously unhappy couple. And, after Ralph's death, any miserable survivor.

Oreos, Fig Newtons, Chips Ahoy!, chocolate wafers, Vienna Fingers. Two large Pepperidge Farm assortments. Graham crackers. Marshmallows. Hershey's bars, Hershey's cocoa, Hershey's syrup, two boxes chocolate pudding, two boxes devil's food cake mix, two bags chocolate chips.

If you create the world as you move through it, I want to say to Stephen sometimes, then doesn't any good thing—any love or happiness or serendipity—have to come from inside you, too?

He would never speak to me again if I did.

"Love," Stephen once told me, when I outrageously

suggested he didn't have to be such a shit to a woman he was breaking up with, over an argument they'd had about a baseball game, "is always subject to authorial revision." He didn't speak to me for six months afterward, because I told him he was just wrong.

"Love," Jamie once told me, annoyed, because I was trying to point out an uncomfortable truth to him, "is different for different people." I'd asked him why it was that Gerri could never clear a week to accompany us on any of the trips, why it was that she disappeared into the bedroom at eight-thirty every night while he sat at the counter with a bottle of wine and a pile of bills. Where it was, exactly, that he thought his tedious martyr routine was going to get him.

"Love can be quiet," he'd said. "Calm. The absence of pain."

Sounds like death to me, I told him.

There's something else Jamie claims not to remember at all; how he could forget it, I can't fathom. The day of Jamie's divorce from Beth, so many years ago, now, it seems like somebody else's life, Ralph was there, waiting outside the courthouse. He'd had his first heart attack not two months before; still, he had the strength to drag himself downtown on his last legs, struggle up the endless steps of the City-County Building, just so he could be there to say to Jamie, as Jamie stepped out of the wide glass doors,

empty-handed, suddenly unmarried, "How come everything you touch turns to shit?"

Kitchen bags, trash bags, heavy-duty Hefties, no pun intended, for the shitter.

It's true my father could be a cruel man. But he was a
man defined by his limitations—something I think I knew
even as a child. And I, unlike Stephen, chose early on not
to let those limitations define me, too.

Ziplocs, large and small, plastic wrap, foil. Rubbermaid
containers. Again. How is it every year we come back with
no lids? I used to have a system, but I gave it up because no
one seemed willing or able to follow it. Fine; if people
want to pay for new containers every year, it makes no
difference to me. I know it's true what Kenneth's always
telling me, though his manner of saying it is inflammatory, offensive, puerile, and graceless: You have to let go of
something.

This is the part I never told Jamie: In that moment, there on
top of the courthouse steps, I decided a few things. I would
never forgive my father for what he had just said. Probably,
I would never get married. Because I loved my brother,
and I hated my father. Because, in our mostly sad and stupid lives, Jamie and I had always stood by each other, and
that's what I would continue to do. And because—of

course I would never say this to Jamie—I've always been just a little better than him, at everything the two of us have ever done.

Ibuprofin, Alka-Seltzer, Band-Aids, gauze. Adhesive tape, duct tape—God-on-a-roll, Ralph always called it, and he could repair anything with it. I myself prefer a half-cent wire bundler, a great invention Ralph didn't live to see. I haven't yet come across a problem I haven't been able to patch together somehow, with one of those.

Ice I'll have to pick up the day we leave. Another thing, amazingly, I can't send anyone else out for. Last year I sent Stephen, mostly to get him to stop asking what he could help me with. Twelve blocks ice. Couldn't be simpler. He came back with crushed. It almost tore his heart to shreds to watch it melting, where I dumped it all, in the corner of the yard.

HOW I WENT (RECIPE FOR LIME CURD)

Gerard comes in and does a pirouette across the kitchen, dancer-toes pointed in his suede bucks, his arms holding a fat column of air that he presents to me upon completing his turn. I decline the air-offering. It looked to me, his bursting from around the corner of the restaurant's dim dining room into the brightly lit kitchen, like an act of birth, Gerard bearing himself from one spot in his existence to another, and I think, what if he wants to take it back? What if he wants to gather up his gesture and undo it, like running a film backward? I don't want to be left in possession of something he might need.

Anyway, I'm working, making the night's desserts for the Blue Heron Bistro. I'm stirring a lime curd, wooden spoon in one hand, whisk in the other. I've turned from the stove to greet Gerard, but I keep stirring, one arm reached in back of me.

"Hey, Green Girl," he says. He's called me that because I'm wearing green pants and a green T-shirt under my apron. Gerard always greets me this way, as if his eyes are attached directly to his mouth: What goes in one place pops right out the other. "Wow, sexy," he says, if I come in for dinner at night, wearing a dress, my hair down: "Rough night?" he asks, if he drops in on a morning after Leon and I have been fighting.

"You're here early," I say. "Are you working lunch?"

"No," Gerard replies, "it's my day off. Actually, I came in to do a little feng shui on my station." He takes a tape measure out of his pocket. "I've got a dangerous corner. I think it's affecting my tips."

"Whatcha making?" he asks, looking over my shoulder, but he turns away before I can answer.

No one here wants to learn how to make anything. "This is delicious," they say, "I always wanted to know how to make this"; or, "I tried it once but I screwed it up."

"It's so easy," I say. But if I start to tell them how to do it, they hold up their hands, begin drifting to other parts of the room.

"Is it the lemon curd?" Gerard asks.

"Lime. You can use either. All you need are six eggs,

eight ounces of lemon or lime juice, and eight ounces of sugar."

"I had a kind-of weird, almost not exactly mystical or magical but maybe you could say fateful experience last night," Gerard says.

"The thing I like about a curd is you can make it when you have practically nothing in the cupboard," I say, turning my face into the steam rising from my *bain-marie.* "What was your weird, fateful experience?"

"I met a guy in the community sauna."

I have a moment of thinking something I've thought about Gerard before, something I've thought about a few of the other people I know: Here is someone I might know forever, or whom I might never see again. I love the shape of Gerard's head, though I've never mentioned this to him—round, with close-cropped hair and ears that stick out. He reminds me of my little brother, who is a man I never see.

"If you do make it, heat up the lime juice first, in a nonreactive saucepan," I say. "It'll cook faster. Why was your experience fateful?"

"I don't know," he says. "I can't explain it."

This is my least favorite explanation for anything.

"I just felt like there was some kind of a connection between us. Something spiritual, almost."

He looks at me as though he's waiting for me to say something. You take your eggs, you take your sugar. You whisk them in a bowl, then pour in the hot juice. Slowly, so the eggs don't cook.

"Could you start a little more at the beginning?" I say.

"Okay," replies Gerard, speaking slowly. "There's this community sauna—have I told you about it?"

"Like, a naked sauna?"

"Yeah," says Gerard, "but it's not like that. There's a real nice energy to it. Everyone's really out front with their stuff."

"What does that *mean*?" I ask. "Out front with their stuff. It sounds like a yard sale." Where does it come from, this vestigial stab of meanness in me? Did it serve some purpose, in another life?

But Gerard just laughs. Once he got mad at me. I had piled a bunch of my things—pint containers of egg whites, chocolate glaze, streusel, a box of limes, a flat of eggs—onto an extra shelf he'd put up on the waiters' side of the fridge.

"You think I put this up for *you*?" he snapped, when he came in for his shift, and I was embarrassed to tell him the truth: I was tired. The night cooks had put their jicama on my dairy shelf, their wonton wrappers, their cilantro oil and chipotle cream, their loose herbs, their veal bones; I was out of space. My divorce was just about to become final, I couldn't get my car to go in reverse, my father was dead, and my mother was thinking of moving to Australia. Yes—for a minute I pretended he'd put the shelf up for me.

"I'm sorry," I say to Gerard, "Tell me about the guy in the sauna." I lift my stainless steel bowl to show him the water barely simmering in the saucepan underneath it. "You want your water bath to be simmering a little bit, or it will take forever, but not too much, or the bottom will scramble." I don't know if he saw, but the steam is burning my fingers, so I drop the bowl back onto the saucepan. "What was he like?"

"Well, I'm not really sure. He was nice, I think. My friend Bridget was sitting here"—Gerard starts arranging pieces of the air with his hands—"and I was sitting here, and when he came in, he had a choice of sitting either here or here, and he chose here. When he looked at me I just felt, I don't know, almost like there was some sort of molecular communication. Not exactly as if we knew each other, but as if our meeting was supposed to happen in just that way, in just that place."

I had that feeling once, I don't tell Gerard. It was just before my life turned into a total disaster.

"You know," Gerard says, "yesterday I woke up with that Move feeling. I had it all day. I almost called you."

"Move feeling?" I say. "Is that some dance thing?"

"Noooo. You know, the Move feeling I was telling you about last week?"

"Oh," I remember. "Like, move: should you or shouldn't you?"

"*Right.* And now, you know, I'm almost sort of thinking, maybe here's my answer."

I look at him blankly.

"That this would be a good reason to decide to stay in a place. You know, meeting a person, and having it be a sign."

"Did you talk to him?"

"Well, not exactly," Gerard says. "But I think he has a cat. I saw his clothes on the bench outside, and his pants had white hairs all over them."

"And do you know if he's gay?"

"I don't know *what* he is. My homometer was totally not picking anything up. He's cute, though."

"Who's cute?" It's Heather, coming around the corner from the dining room into the kitchen. That corner is a hazard: You can't hear people lurking behind it. I'm glad I wasn't telling Gerard about the vegetarian chili she made for the take-out deli upstairs the other day. It was so bad, I took some home for Leon to try.

"Try to name one spice that's not in this," I said to Leon.

"Ummm," he said, squinching his forehead at the taste of it. "Cinnamon."

"Nope."

"Nutmeg."

"Try something harder."

"Cardamom."

"Nope."

"Dill."

"That's an herb. But, nope."

"This guy at the sauna," Gerard is saying to Heather.

"Oh, cool," she replies. Everything's cool with her, or else *Right on*. Which is how, I guess, the cardamom got in the chili in the first place. That chili was inedible, but still, I can't keep from admiring her sureness.

"What are you making?" Heather asks me.

"Lime curd," I say. "You have to stir it constantly with a wooden spoon or a heat-proof spatula. It should start to thicken in about five minutes, or when the mixture reaches a hundred and seventy degrees."

"Cool," she says.

What got Gerard and me started on the whole moving conversation was that I told him a couple of months ago I was going to move away from Massachusetts. "As soon as my divorce goes through. Don't tell anyone, though."

"You are?" he said with surprise. "Why?"

"I don't know," I answered. "Because I was only planning to stay in the East one year, but it's been nine. Because I haven't seen the sun for thirty-six days. Because every time I come here the top of the lemon juicer's in a different place and my ramekins are filled with chopped garlic and rubber bands. Because my therapist's an old lady, and the other day when I went to her house to drop off some tapes, she came to the door without any teeth."

"Where are you moving?" he asked.

"Mmm. West. Utah, maybe. That's where I'm from."

"Huh," Gerard said. "Strange. I never thought of you as being from somewhere."

"I'm not even sure if Gary will let Katrin come with me, though," I said.

"Oh," said Gerard, "that's hard." Then he said, "I think about moving West. As a matter-of-fact, I had an interesting experience there once."

"What was it?" I can't remember what I was making while we were having this conversation—maybe flan, something else I like because it only has a few ingredients in it. I like to tell people that's one of the reasons I'm a good baker, because of what I can do without: I can bake without flour, I can bake without eggs, I can bake without milk, cream, butter, sugar, chocolate. Just not all at once.

"Well," said Gerard, "I was visiting my friend Cheyenne in Tempe, and we were goofing around one night, well, not exactly goofing, and I just happened, totally out of the blue, to channel this very old spirit-being type of person."

"Did it have a name?" I asked. "She? He?" I didn't know if this was the right question, but his remark made me remember a conversation I'd overheard once in cooking school, in which three of my new friends had discovered that their guardian angels all had the same name.

"Actually," said Gerard, "his name was Tomequiu."

"Oh," I said, feeling lonely.

"He was a very, very ancient person, and he gave me some map coordinates."

"Did you go there?"

"No," Gerard said. "But I looked them up. They were in the desert. He told me he lived in a sort-of cave, beneath a mountain-like landform. And he gave me, almost, an understanding, that when I found this place, I would be able to lose all my fear and hesitation and jump into this cave-like hole and be okay."

That was the day I told him I'd been doing some reading about the Donner party.

"I've always been kind of fascinated with them," I told Gerard. "I mean, maybe more than normal people are."

"A lot of people don't think about the Donner party at all," is what my husband said, long ago, when I tried to explain it to him.

I don't know why I'm so interested in them. The eating is what springs to most people's minds, but not mine. It's the other things I like to think about: the moving, for example—leaving their homes for the unknown, traveling so far. And the *choosing*: Go the slow way and most likely survive, or save three hundred miles by the fateful cut-off? Walk out into the snow to look for the rescue party and die of exposure, or wait at camp and starve to death?

Also, I like the word "party." The way it used to mean something in between strangers and a family, a word to use if you're talking about people who aren't exactly either. People whose lives, for one long, accidental moment, hang suspended with yours over the spectacular, terrible landscape.

———

"Did you ever think maybe you were there?" Gerard said, that day.

"Were where?" said Heather, coming around the corner. She'd come in early to make hummus for the deli. She likes to make two flavors, regular and black bean, and create a yin-yang design with them on the platter.

"Nowhere," I said, at the same moment Gerard said, "With the Donner party."

"Oh," she said, puzzled but not interested. "Were they the twelve pain-in-the-butts that came in on Saturday night?"

"No, silly," said Gerard, and he was about to tell her, but I cut him off.

"What did you do this morning, Heather?" I asked her.

"Oh, it was so beautiful out, I spent the morning chillin' with Aldo Leopold and John Muir in the backyard."

"Wooo," said Gerard. "Who're they?"

"Dead guys," I said, and she looked at me funny, then turned her back to me.

"They're *just*, like," she said to Gerard, "the two original forestry dudes."

"So, Heather," Gerard says.

"Dude."

"Did you hear that I'm thinking of moving?"

"Get outta town!" she says. "Far out!"

"Well, Abby got me interested in the idea," he tells her, smiling at me, "but then it started to seem like the idea was actually already there in a way, and then everything just started saying, 'Move. Move.' "

"Where are you moving?" Heather asks.

"It's the funniest thing," Gerard tells her, "but everything seems to be saying, 'Utah.' My crystals are saying it, my house plants are saying it, even the cats are saying it. It's not a place I ever particularly thought of before, but once Abby mentioned it, it's weird, it's like some sort of action or force or maybe you could call it cosmic energy got set into motion."

"Your cats are saying, 'Utah'?" I ask. Why don't I ever get a clear sign like that, I want to know.

"I was in Utah once," Heather says. "Just passing through. I wanted to get a drink and play some pool, but it just wasn't happening."

A thought is forming in my head, but I know I won't tell Gerard: Maybe he and I could be roommates. Maybe we could get a house together. A duplex, maybe. Maybe my brother could come up from Florida and live with us. Even though I haven't talked to him in many years, I remember him as a nice kid. Maybe if Heather passed through again, we could convince her to stay awhile.

Leon would want to move, too. He wants to marry me. He was the one who found us the therapist, the old lady. "This really seems to be working!" Leon would say, week after week, and I didn't tell him how I spent most of each session looking at her, realizing she was even older than I'd decided she was the week before.

"Utah," Heather is saying. "I don't know, dude." She's finished the hummus; now she's pouring sesame oil into a big stainless-steel bowl.

"Yeah," says Gerard, "I don't know, either."

"What do you mean, you don't know?" I say.

I've been thinking about what Gerard said about the Donner party. Up until now, whenever I'd play "What would you come back as?" with someone, I'd choose to be a forty-niner: just some guy traveling alone around the West, maybe seeing places no one had ever seen before, starting a town and naming it after myself, getting drunk off the bee-wack that rose to the top of my sourdough.

But I like the idea Gerard gave me.

If I'd been in the Donner party, maybe I would have had a bunch of kids.

Maybe I was mourning the recent tragic death of my husband, the passing of a loved one being just the impetus to hit the road.

Maybe I was filled with a sense of expectation. Perhaps I was not as ordinary as I seemed, as afraid as I looked.

And even though in the end, their choices weren't that great, I have a feeling the Donners didn't just sit around camp thinking about it that way. I know they believed in

God, for instance, though I've never been quite sure how that all works. And some days, I know from books I've read, one or another of them would wake up and look around, and even though each day their plight was worse than the day before, write in his or her journal, "Fine morning. Clear and pleasant. The snow looks delightful after the long storm."

I remember something important. "You have to remember to tare," I say. Heather glances over at me, then back to her Asian curried tabouli and Kalamata salad, which, from the looks of it, is about to acquire large cubes of cheddar.

"Tare-my-hair," says Gerard. I'm going to have to convert to volume measurements for them, I can see. How many home cooks own a kitchen scale?

"Eggs count as liquid," I say, "so eight ounces is a cup, and the same for the lemon juice, but sugar is different."

I wait for someone to ask me why. I've been waiting for the moment I can get the pound bag of bay leaves, big as a couch pillow, out of dry storage and set it next to a pound of butter, watch their disbelief.

"Eight ounces of sugar is about one cup plus two tablespoons," I say. "I can tell you what I mean by 'tare,' if you'd like."

"Try this salad," says Heather. "Tell me if it needs more brown sugar." She gives me a spoonful, stands close, watches me chew. Heather's a large woman—tall, taut, and

strong. She's the one people go to when they need something opened, something lifted, something reached.

She has a sister; I suddenly remember that. A twin, almost indistinguishable from her, according to reports, and I
always have a hard time picturing it—imagining the two of
them, together, creating a weight that might throw the
earth off balance, just by sitting together and giggling, or
combing their hair in the same mirror.

"Pretty good?" Heather says; she's on her way out of
the kitchen before I can nod, cheese in cheek.

"Catch ya on the upside," Heather says, carrying her
salad away, like a big baby, on her hip. If Heather were in
the Donner party, I think, watching her strong back round
the corner, she'd be the last one alive. If anyone could plow
through those mountains to California, it'd be Heather.
Living off her body fat, carrying the baby, the combined
heat of the three of them, Heather, her sister, and the baby,
melting a path through the ten-foot drifts.

"Look," I say to Gerard, but he's turned and begun walking
away. The curd's almost done, and I'm really wishing that
just this once, someone would stick around to see the
whole thing.

When the mixture starts to thicken, you have to pay attention. There's a moment: not before, not after, but—this
is what I can't explain, this is the reason I want people to

make it themselves—not itself, either. Maybe it's a moment beside itself, a moment outside of time. Maybe it's a moment of *knowing*—like jumping into a cave, or setting off across snowy mountains.

"Look," I say again, and Gerard turns back at the sound of my voice. "When it seems like something's about to happen, grab your whisk. You want to move the mixture, but not aerate it, because the more air you add, the less you'll be able to see. You want to be able to see."

"I want to be able to see my wine key," he says, rooting through the waiters' credenza.

Suddenly I remember the truth, from when I was a Donner.

The truth is, I had no children. I was a sturdy, plain-looking woman of thirty-eight, and I was all alone. When I saw the notice, COMPANY FORMING, I sold everything I had and headed West. When we got hung up at the lake, I shared my provisions with the families who were running low, though I felt no one ever really liked me. No one ever stopped at my cabin to visit, asked me what I intended to do when I got to California, what I had left behind.

Also, I'll admit it, I did partake of one of the party. I chose to eat a man, because I had never touched one, and I was curious.

"If you want to, you can add butter when it's done," I tell Gerard, but he's pirouetting away, undoing our connection. "Up to six ounces, room temperature. I never do, though. I like it better without. And then, actually, it's a fairly low-fat dessert. Put plastic wrap on the surface, so it doesn't form a skin.

"What are you doing now?" I ask him.

"Oh," he says. "I'm going to go fool around on the Internet. I met a guy named Duane on-line who's been giving me all sorts of tips on what it's like to be gay in Utah. He says I can stay with him and his wife when I get there."

I don't remember how I finally went, but I do remember this: I was one of the ones who got sick of waiting for the rescue party and set out over the mountains. Come on, I said, to anyone who could still stand up, but no one followed me.

It snowed so hard that when I woke up the first morning I was buried two feet under, except for my face, which I'd woken to brush off several times in the night. But the snow had stopped and the morning was spectacular, the valley around me one unbroken bowl of glittering whiteness.

"Bye," says Gerard, "see ya Friday," and he's gone. Neither he nor Heather let me tell them about the scale. It's not crucial to the outcome. But I like to tare. Every time you add an ingredient, set the scale back to zero. That way there's no addition or subtraction, nothing to forget. Turn the little dial on the front, six eggs become weightless. Add your sugar, set the scale to zero again. Lime juice. Each time, start with nothing. It's just a little trick to keep from getting confused, but I like to think of each ingredient as a new beginning. Or a last memory, like waking up another day, miraculously—terrifyingly—not dead yet, searching the landscape for a trace of something human, getting ready to decide where, in that whole valleyful of white, to place a foot.

INVERSION

The Chinese kids are the only ones with ordinary first names: Alice Fang, Kathy Yuan, Andrew and Elizabeth Zhou. The other kids have names like Katrin's, Abby sees, as she studies the program—ethnic, variant, connotative, *interesting*, the mellifluent syllables of the surnames of strangers. No one but Abby herself knows that she regrets Katrin's name, chosen from a book in a moment she thinks of, now, as similar to a trip to the mall. Of course, she'd found a rarefied little shop not everyone knew about, rummaged deep through an obscure bin for something interesting but not *out there,* like but not *alike.* Little did she know this shop would soon start to advertise, hold a big sale.

Abby folds her program and twists in her seat, tries to see the mountains through the reflective glass doors of the music store. They had been slowly disappearing behind a blanket of white smog as Abby, Katrin, and Leon drove the long distance on the freeway to get to the recital.

The smog has been getting worse for days. Haze, the newspapers and TV news call it, as if the stew of pollution filling the valley is a mere visual disturbance.

Every morning, before Leon and Katrin are awake, Abby goes out onto the porch to check the conditions, to see if any storms have come along in the night to blow the poisons on to the next place. But there's no relief forecast, no bad weather to lighten her spirits, and each day she goes inside with a feeling of unease, starts Katrin's oatmeal, and stands at the kitchen window staring out, willing the still leaves of the trees to move.

It had been nearly dark when they pulled into the Piano World parking lot. The music store is in a part of the city that didn't exist when Abby was growing up here, twenty-five years earlier. That's what she'd thought as she drove, searching for something for her eyes to rest on besides brick, metal, asphalt, cable, vinyl, concrete, neon, colored plastic. You couldn't even say, this used to be farmland:

squat ranches at the edges of sprawling, scruffy fields; big cottonwoods lining the banks of irrigation ditches; the foothills of the Wasatch turning pink, then blue at the end of the day. You could only say, this is another place now. A place without a memory, one that blared out names at her: House of Fabric, Crown Burger, Del's, Sofa City, Los Hermanos, Duane's Discount, Staff of Life Bread Company, Safeway, Bar None Bootery, Vera's, Ed's, Dix's, Dean's, Muffler King, Cost City, Pet World, Tire World, Soccer World, Discount World, Mattress World, all the different worlds.

They were the first ones there, Abby saw, as they entered the store, besides Katrin's teacher, Jia Li and Jia Li's daughter, Julie. Jia Li and Julie were in the back, unpacking grocery bags.

All Abby knows about Jia Li and Julie's life is that Julie's father, Jia Li's husband, died five years ago, of cancer; and that they live in a dark split-level ranch not far from here.

"Oh, hi!" called Jia Li when she saw them. "We're just setting up the refreshments."

"Let me help," Abby said, though she saw, as she took a grocery bag from Julie, there wasn't much to do. The refreshments were big bags of cheese puffs, pretzels, popcorn, and potato chips, a few boxes of crackers, a jar of peanuts.

"Nothing to drink," said Jia Li apologetically, "I hope

it's okay. Last year there was a problem—someone left an orange soda on top of one of the pianos and it spilled inside."

"Come on," Julie said to Katrin, and Katrin followed her into the maze of pianos. The pianos, mostly grands, arranged tightly and at all different angles, made Abby think of a squat, shiny forest. Each one was polished to a high luster, the colors and grains of the woods conspicuous in their uniqueness. Julie and Katrin sat down at one, and their heads disappeared behind its shiny, propped-open lid.

Abby watches Jia Li, who is standing at the door, now, greeting the other people who have started to arrive. She touches everyone, Abby notices—a hand to the arm or shoulder, a hug if it's a child. The children, business-like, hand their parents their coats and head off into the pianos to practice.

Disconnected bits of music begin to rise into the air. From within the din, Abby can hear phrases of Katrin's pieces, floating up, then disappearing. Momentarily, she imagines the notes as words, the clear, melodic emanations as her daughter's voice, speaking to her in a language she doesn't understand.

"How's your daughter's piano coming along?" asks a man who's sat down a few seats from Abby. They've met in Jia Li's driveway; he's the father of a boy named Micah, whose lesson is scheduled before Katrin's on Thursday afternoons.

"Fine," Abby replies.

Micah's father is holding a baby. Abby feels a reflexive worry and doesn't know why, then she remembers the air. It can't be good for a baby to breathe.

"Micah's really become very serious, working with Jia Li," the man says. Abby nods, smiles blankly.

She looks around for Leon and sees him on the other side of the room, inspecting the pianos. The first piano Abby looked at when she walked in had an engraved card propped on it: $13,750, it said. $8,075, said the one next to it. She couldn't resist putting both hands on a gleaming walnut Steinway and running them over its curved sides, knowing before she saw its price—$27,000—that it was the most valuable thing in the room.

When Abby met Leon, his one-room apartment had been full of instruments and equipment: a keyboard, amplifier, microphone, a flute, a horn, a couple of guitars propped in the corner.

"You're a musician," she'd said, surprised, the first time she visited. He'd never mentioned it.

"I play some," he'd corrected her. "Badly." She'd never heard him, though. Once, when she'd come in without knocking, he'd been sitting with his back to her at the keyboard. But there was no sound in the room, and for a second, she'd been confused—his shoulders were moving slightly. She'd thought maybe he was crying, until she realized he was playing with headphones on.

Leon has paused, now, and is peering behind a luminous black upright. She and Leon used to talk, sometimes, about having a baby, though they haven't since they moved here. He's been busy getting his business off the ground.

From her study on the third floor of their house, she can see, on a clear day, all the way to the west side of the valley, where Leon's "office"—a small corrugated aluminum warehouse from within which, according to Leon's projections, will soon rise a sound-insulation empire, a source of untold riches and success—lies. On a bad day, though, there's nothing there, just whiteness beyond the roof of the house next door.

"Excuse me," Micah's father says, and he stands up. Abby follows his gaze. Across the room, Micah has stopped practicing and is standing next to one of the other students, watching him play. Micah's father smiles stiffly at Abby and heads toward the two boys.

Abby checks her watch. Jia Li is holding the door open, ushering in one last family. They don't even have a child— why are they here? Abby wonders; then she sees that one of them is, actually, a boy, older than the other children— sixteen or seventeen, maybe. Jia Li's face lights up. She pats the back of the boy's puffy brown parka, says something in his ear. She obviously favors him. Abby feels slightly annoyed; she feels her annoyance extending to the whole family—the mother and father, too, who have come in so late and can't seem to get their coats off and arranged and sit down in their chairs. Some of the parents seem to possess such a large sense of entitlement. Showing up whenever they want to, taking up Jia Li's whole driveway with their huge vehicles, chatting with her past their time to leave, as if their forty dollars an hour buys more of her than everyone else's forty dollars an hour.

"Okay," Jia Li says loudly, and she claps her hands. The children start to drift over to the performance area. Now there is just the sound of one set of notes being played. Micah hasn't noticed that everyone else has stopped. Nor has his father, who is standing next to him with the baby, and the sound of Micah's playing seems odd, suddenly—frightening, like a wailing voice. Like something Abby suddenly remembers: the moment after an accident she once saw—two cars colliding in the intersection in front of her house. The crash of metal on metal, a silence, then a child starting to cry. Abby was twelve years old. Her father had gotten the child out of the car and sat down on the curb, trying to comfort it. The part that had never left Abby, though—that had given her the creeps—was the way the adults were acting. Dazed, bloody, injured, they had struggled out of their cars and were wandering around. One woman had opened her door, shaken off Abby's mother's staying hand, and said, "I have to go to work," then staggered to the curb and fallen down.

Micah's fingers hit wrong notes, and he stops.

"Jesus Christ!" Abby thinks she hears his father hiss.

Micah, looking up and realizing the situation, stands and crosses the room, leaving his father to make his way to his seat. Jia Li smiles and takes Micah by both shoulders, leads him to a chair.

Katrin, who is sitting in the second row with Abby and Leon, tugs at Abby's shoulder and whispers, "Can I change my seat?"

"Sure," Abby says. She watches, surprised, as Katrin sidles around the row of chairs and sits down in the empty seat next to Micah's. She thought Katrin didn't like Micah. Katrin whispers something in Micah's ear. Micah whispers back. Katrin nods.

"Mackenzie Kirchner," Jia Li says, introducing the first performer. The program says Mackenzie is six. With a self-possession Abby envies, Mackenzie walks to the piano, climbs onto the bench and, begins, slowly, to play her one simple piece.

Across from her, Abby sees, Mackenzie's father is slowly, excruciatingly dying. Abby wishes she could tell him she's sure Mackenzie isn't going to make a mistake. The look on Mackenzie's face reminds Abby of Katrin's first recital. Katrin, also six, had chosen a loud, challenging piece, though she'd only had a few lessons, and—the word that still comes to Abby's mind is—*dispensed* with it. Abby remembers thinking, as soon as Katrin had finished her piece, laid aside the fierce concentration she'd mustered for her task, and turned to look for her, that the performance boded well, that this was a quality that would stand her daughter in good stead in life: the ability to approach a worrisome problem and put it away cleanly and neatly.

One by one the children play. Tiny, unsmiling Elizabeth Zhou removes a pair of white gloves and lays them in her mother's lap before walking to the stage. She has chosen a technical tour de force; Abby marvels at her miniature fingers flying, crossing over each other, replacing each other on the keys. When she stops, the air feels full of silence.

Elizabeth's older brother Andrew's pieces sound the same, only faster. When Andrew finishes, Abby whispers to Leon, "That was impressive, wasn't it?" When he doesn't answer, she turns slightly; his arched eyebrows and cool look jab at her. She shouldn't have hazarded this opinion of Andrew Zhou's playing. Leon, after all, knows much more about music than she does. There is little he likes. Abby isn't allowed to buy him CDs or tapes. "Save your money," he says. When she first knew him she'd buy tickets to concerts, sometimes, but she quickly grew discouraged at her inability to discern what was worth going to and what wasn't.

"Let's leave," he'd say, twenty minutes into a performance, standing abruptly. On the rare occasions he liked something, he'd say of the performer, only, "He has soul." He still wouldn't want to stay. "She had soul," he'd say, his face expressionless, on the way out, as if they were conducting a soul census, attending the concert to determine that one thing and then leave.

"He was okay," Leon says now, as Andrew Zhou walks back to his seat. Abby turns around to see if Andrew's mother heard.

Katrin is next. As she walks to the stage, Leon takes Abby's hand and squeezes it tight.

When Katrin started taking lessons, Leon had taken charge of renting a piano, going from showroom to showroom, bartering with the salesmen, scouring the classifieds, phoning movers and tuners.

"Play," Katrin said to him, as soon as the movers had gone. He'd hesitated a moment, then sat down at the keyboard and played a few jazzy chords, then he'd stood up again.

"No," he'd said. "I'll tell you a story, though. When I was a little kid, I had a miniature organ that my dad taught me to play. It had two keyboards, one on top and one on the bottom, and I'd play and pump the foot pedals and sing, like a little one-man band.'

Katrin plays four pieces, doesn't make any major mistakes. Abby can feel the energy slowly leaving Leon's hand, his grip slackening for every piece Katrin gets past. Katrin looks over at Abby when she's finished. Any emotion on her face, besides relief, is undetectable.

When it's Micah's turn to play, Abby is surprised: He isn't as good as she thought he'd be. Or else he's chosen easy pieces. When Micah positions his fingers on the keyboard, his father looks as though something has entered his body and is trying to find a way out. He leans forward as Micah's playing gets louder, hunches down as it decrescendos, something appears to be struggling in his throat when Micah stumbles near the end of his last piece. Micah, when he is finished, sits very still, like a pond swallowing a stone.

Julie is second to last. Her pieces are difficult, complicated. As soon as she plays the last notes, Leon leans over and whispers to Abby, "She's going to be a teacher, just like her mother." Abby turns to look at him. "*Shut* up," she wants to say.

Abby herself can't tell whether Julie's playing was soulful or merely competent—she's always had trouble telling the difference. Usually she guesses wrong. She tries to imagine Julie three or four years old—the age she'd been when Jia Li started her at piano. She wonders if Julie's father had been sick by then. If he had lain in a room nearby and let the sounds wash over him and understood, this was what he had, all he had: the notes stumbling through the air, the small, black-haired girl in the pink afternoon light—this one moment, precisely carved out of the time he had left, and nothing more.

The large boy, Jason, is last on the program. He is dressed oddly, in clothes that make him look more adult than child: slacks, sweater vest, big, shiny loafers. Leon looks at Abby and smirks as Jason shambles up to the piano. Abby is about to tell Leon, really, to just shut up, but when he speaks, there's something in his voice. Affection, possibly.

"Big Jason," he says. "Bring it on home, buddy." Jason smiles on his way to the piano. He is the only one of the children who's smiled, and the effect is bizarre, as if he's going to play a trick on the audience. Jason's parents sit close to the door, still as animals sniffing the wind.

Jason settles himself and turns to look at Jia Li, then he turns back to the piano and bangs his hands down in the opening chords of his piece. The notes are jarringly wrong. Abby feels the air turn electric. Jason raises his eyebrows, picks up his hands, and poises them over the piano again. Gets himself ready—to get it wrong again or to get it right; Abby sees that, unlike the other children, he's not sure. In front of her, Jia Li is whispering urgently to him: "G-flat. Left hand, G-flat. Right hand D-flat, E-flat, A." Seized with a moment of confidence, or something else, he plunges his hands down again, wrong. He turns to the audience, smiles apologetically. Then, without looking, he tries again. To his own surprise, he gets it right; he is off and flying. He crashes through the piece, swaying, leaning into the keyboard, shaking his head. When he presses his hands into the piece's final chord, he smiles and closes his eyes, lifts his face to some imagined light.

"Wow," Abby says to Leon.

Leon nods. "He's got soul," he says. Then he adds, flippantly, "Better than doing drugs. It'll keep him off the streets." Abby pulls back, looks at him. This inscrutable man she's found herself with. His mother once showed her some snapshots of Leon, small, big-eyed, smiling, in cowboy pajamas. Abby is trying to remember them, now. She is trying to picture him small. Playing, singing. A little one-man band. But she can't do it, she can't pull the memory— one she doesn't even possess, anyway—of the little boy out of the man in front of her.

Jason stands up, takes his bow, then heads for the snack table. All the tension is gone, now, the air turned flabby with the parents' exhalations, the release of the children's taut limbs. Murmuring, the adults rise, turn around, stretch, then everyone begins to move toward the small table and its salty snacks.

The children are already there, chattering and filling their fists with pretzels, potato chips, peanuts. Abby can't see Katrin, and, for a moment, she worries. She drifts around the outside of the room until she finds her, sitting on a puffy piano bench next to Micah, their heads bent close together. Abby can't see what they're doing. It looks like Micah is offering Katrin something to eat, feeding her. But when Abby gets close, she sees they are only talking. Katrin is delineating something in the air in front of her face with her hands—some imaginary object—and Micah is looking at it, smiling and nodding and tracing something on its surface with a fingertip.

"Hey," Abby says, nearing them; they both look up at

her at once. Stupid, Abby thinks, too late. She thought she could enter the moment. The two children look at her blankly.

"There's snacks," she says lamely, and she heads, alone, toward the table.

Jia Li comes up beside Abby, touches her elbow. They stand, surveying the crowd. At the snack table, Jason is leading the other children in a game of throwing Chee•tos in the air and catching them in their upturned mouths.

"He's a good boy," Jia Li says, as if Abby has spoken out loud. She has been watching Jason. His parents, who, as far as Abby can tell, haven't talked to anyone all evening, stand apart from everyone else, near one of the pianos. Probably thinking about whether or not they want to buy it.

"It's too bad," Jia Li says.

"What is?" asks Abby.

"He started only two years ago. He loves to play, but he will never be good."

"Why not?" asks Abby.

"Because it's too late," Jia Li says, as if the answer's obvious, though her voice is gentle. "It's tragic, really," she adds.

"Tragic?" repeats Abby; she hears the challenge in her voice. If the boy enjoys playing, if his parents are willing to fork over for lessons so that he can be happy . . .

"He's had kind of a hard life," Jia Li says.

Yes, Abby thinks impatiently. Life is hard. So they'll never be able to buy their big, clumsy son what he doesn't have: talent. But he's got soul. An untradeable commodity, but still.

"Two years ago," says Jia Li, "they were living in their car."

Katrin is suddenly standing between them. Jia Li puts an arm around her shoulder.

"I'm thirsty, Mom," Katrin says.

"No drinks," Jia Li says. "It's bad."

"Oh, no," says Abby, but a funny thing happens as she says it: Micah comes over to where his father is standing, near them, and says, "I'm thirsty, Dad," and at that moment, Leon appears.

"Think we ought to go soon?" he asks. A general movement has begun, toward coats, toward the door. Maybe everyone's gotten thirsty at once, Abby thinks, like a herd of human animals.

She cringes as she steps into the parking lot—she'd forgotten about the air. "Hurry and get in," she says to Katrin, and hustles her into the car. Only the tops of the mountains to the south are now still visible; to the west, she sees nothing. Abby squints to try and coax a ridge, a shadow, any contour at all out of the thick, dark sky.

———

She hadn't seen Jason and his family say good-bye to anyone; they are walking, now, away from the half-full parking
lot, up the sidewalk of the bright, deserted strip.

"I wonder where they live," she says. "I wonder if they
need a ride."

The air in every direction is white. Wherever you are
in the inversion, Abby knows, you feel like you're standing in the one pocket of clear air, and you feel, in some
shameful way, safe in that fragile oasis, graced. Though it
isn't true. They're in the middle of it, she knows. Breathing
poison.

"Yes," she says, "let's see if they need a ride," but Katrin
says, "They're gone." It's true—it's as if the white haze just
swallowed them up.

"Mom," Katrin says, suddenly, urgently, "I'm starving
thirsty!" Abby and Leon smile at each other.

"Me, too," Leon says.

"We'll get you a drink as soon as we see a place," Abby
tells her. That's one thing she's pretty sure she'll be able
to find out here without a problem—something cold and
sweet for Katrin.

TO SARAH, WHEREVER YOU ARE

I was baking a lemon cake the other day when I thought of you. Maybe it was all those eggs, thirty of them lined up in their flat, that made me remember the last couple of weeks of the year I spent in San Francisco. The year I left five-year-old Katrin with her father, the year of school and distance and trying, through force of will, to get my life, like a big vehicle I didn't know how to steer, to turn in a different direction. A year of knowing you were just across town, though you were too busy to see me much. But sometimes it made me feel a little better, to imagine you in your apartment on the other end of Divisadero, making a cup of coffee, ironing an outfit. Coming in the door at night and shuffling through the mail, switching on your answering machine, maybe hearing the sound of my voice.

It was a year of curious, untethered feelings. I would ride the bus, weekends, alone, not going anywhere in particular, just trying to produce an experience, over and over again—I liked looking up from my book, somewhere on a randomly chosen route, to find myself in a place I'd never been before, hear my voice say, softly, the far-fetched names of its coordinates: "Edinburgh and Amazon, Persia and Peru."

It was also the year a giant sinkhole opened up and swallowed a street in Sea Cliff. I clipped the newspaper picture and kept it in the cardboard box on the floor that served as my desk, and every once in a while I'd get it out and look at it. The ground had just yawned open in the hazy, white daylight and swallowed a house, and part of another, a piece of road, some giant palms.

I rode my bike up the day after it happened and stood looking over the edge. I stood a long time, understanding the way something had been there, and now was gone, and I wished that I'd brought you with me, though it wasn't the kind of thing you'd have had time for. But I thought maybe you'd understand, too, or be fascinated, like I was, at the way the caved-in hole looked—not like a bit of temporary damage, which would eventually be repaired, even though, I'd heard, the city planned to fill it with garbage—

but like something different. A changed place. A place where nothingness had carved out a home for itself, an absence that had become the present.

Sometimes I ask Katrin if she remembers you. "My friend Sarah, from a long time ago. You met her once in Salt Lake City when you were about two," I say. Katrin's eight now, by the way.

"Hmm," she says, "I don't think so. Wait, was she the one whose mom used to say that thing?" She only knows you from stories I've told.

" 'Hell's bells!' " your mother would yell when she got mad. It used to scare me, I told Katrin, but I also had to try really hard not to laugh. " *'Hell's bells,* Sarah!' " You were always in trouble; I told Katrin that. All your mom had to do was see you and she'd start yelling. I'd try to disappear, sneak back to your room till it was over. I told Katrin about your room, your canopy bed, the gold and white vanity with its wire-backed tuffet, the pictures of the big-eyed girl and boy.

"Tell me more," Katrin would say. I could touch the surface of that time anywhere, it seemed, and come up with a handful of details that would sound to Katrin like a story: "Sarah had a gigantic closet, the kind you can walk right into, and inside that closet were . . ."

"Sarah drove a huge junker car and I sat in the passenger

seat, and my seat was broken, so we tied it to the dashboard, through the heating vent, with string . . ."

"Sarah and I had a raft," I told Katrin. Do you remember? "The kind you blow up. We kept it in the trunk of her car, and whenever we saw a good river, we'd stop and take it out and go floating down."

Katrin came home the other day and asked me, "Mom, what's 'coming of age'?" and the first thing I thought of was you; I wondered what you would tell her. You and I talked about it once, inebriated, in Boston. "It's not about sex," we both agreed. It wasn't about turning from girls into women, not exactly. It's not about what people tell you it is, I don't think, I said to you that night.

Would you have thought of Sewing I, the first semester of seventh grade? The first three weeks of class, before we got started on our appliquéd pillows, our embroidered Raggedy Anns with outfits (or, in my case, the mere dumbfounded witnessing of Merrilee Monson's camel-hair coat taking shape), we were taught something called Health and Personal Hygiene, a kind of mortifying etiquette. Just in case learning to inhabit our new, thirteen-year-old selves wasn't discomfitting enough, Miss Shumlin would stand up there daily—remember her smooth, sadistic voice, her cruel quips, her hypothetical misfit teen, "Becky Sue Goodbody," who tried hard but never got anything right?—listing our new responsibilities: We needed to take daily showers, wash our hair, shave our legs, apply astringents to our pimples, use deodorant; douche—horrors—if our mothers approved; we needed to remember to change our tampons and not flush sanitary napkins down the toilet ("You *know* who unclogs those toilets, right? *Men!*") and that, whereas up until now we had been treasured beings, our smooth, limber bodies the objects of our parents' pride and our own pleasure, now, except for our extreme, constant vigilance, we would be offensive to others. We looked dirty and exuded disgusting substances; people would be able to smell us coming.

You wouldn't have told Katrin any of that, would you?

"Maybe," I said to Katrin, "it's a moment when you go from feeling one way about the world to feeling another way." As soon as I said it, though, I wished I hadn't. The look on her face was terrible.

"But, I mean, what *happens*?" she asked.

"I don't know," I finally told her. "I can't remember."

It's not that I don't remember things from that time. I can tell you intimate details about the girl I was, then: which were her favorite articles of clothing and who she was with when she bought each one; I can remember, physically, the fit of her jeans, the way her favorite black turtleneck hugged her middle and just met the flat waistband of her white corduroys, the feel of her feet in opaque tights, slipping around inside wooden clogs. I remember what she kept in her room and where; every phase her hair had been through; the smell of Flex conditioner lingering around her head like a protective cloud; the names of the boys she liked who didn't like her back; the ones she didn't like, who liked her. I could pinpoint every spot on her skin where one of them had ever touched her, by accident or on purpose.

I can even remember her best friend's wardrobe, the ten white turtlenecks that looked the same, but fit uniquely; the smell of the best friend's avocado-and-cucumber lotion; every bathing suit the best friend had ever owned and in what order; the exact shade of her best friend's skin after lying in the sun for four hours.

Do you remember the summer we spent sneaking into every hotel, motel, condo, and country club pool in town?

"If anyone asks, tell them your dad's a doctor and he's at a conference and you're staying in room 406 or something," you told me as we pulled into the Little America parking lot that first time. I was supposed to be the "smart" one, valedictorian of junior high, but, I only saw much later, I depended on you to tell me everything: what to wear, how to do my hair, what to eat, what words to use, what boys to like, who to be friends with.

"You can't say 406 if the hotel only has two floors," you told me, thinly hidden exasperation in your voice as we hopped barefoot, banished, across the hot asphalt a few minutes later. You were wearing a goldenrod Hang Ten bikini with curving seams over the boobs; that I thought it was hideous was, I knew, just my own failure of vision.

"Does it hurt?" Katrin asked.

"Does what hurt?"

"Coming of age," she said. That's what you need a child in your life for, to say things like that.

"No," I told her.

Wouldn't you have lied, too?

Katrin offered me some advice last week. We were walking home from the market. February in Massachusetts. I was looking around inside myself for the energy it was going to take to walk up the stairs and slice the avocado I'd bought for her dinner. "I feel awful, Kat," I said. I figured it would be better—less random and scary—if I could slip the words out before the tears that were threatening to leak out of the corners of my eyes.

"Why do you feel awful?" she asked, and I said the first thing that came into my head, not what I'd been thinking, but something I thought she could understand. But, also, I realized as soon as I said it, the truth.

"I wish I had some friends," I told her. "A friend. It's been a long time since I had a really good friend. Do you know what I mean?"

"But Mom," she said, "you have friends," and she went down the list: my new boyfriend, who I was taking a little time off from; her father, who only wanted to talk to me about practical matters; our neighbors Steve and Sue, who had just had a baby; my mother; the mothers of her school friends.

"Yeah," I said. "Yeah, you're right, I do."

"I know what you mean, though, Mom," she said. Then she said, "Maybe you should have an imaginary friend."

When she said it, Sarah, something happened: A memory rushed out of me as if from a closed-off room—a memory of something I'd wanted to tell you about as soon as it happened, because I knew that the moment was being given to me like a gift, and I wanted to be able to understand it perfectly. But, not having told you, I'd forgotten it completely.

One day about four or five years ago, when Gary and I were still married, I was at one of his softball games with Katrin, and sitting next to me in the bleachers was the daughter of one of his colleagues. Hannah. She'd been nine or ten when I'd last seen her; quite a while had passed, and she had really changed. She'd become so pretty. Her face had lost its childlike openness, and her eyes, dark and hooded, seemed to contain some private knowledge, though I couldn't imagine what it was. Also, she'd grown breasts, gotten hips. "Blossomed" is a word people sometimes use to describe such a change; when the word came into my mind, I realized how appalling it was. She wasn't a plant.

Hannah had been charged with watching her half-sister, Charlotte, who's Katrin's age. We sat side by side, watching Charlotte and Katrin run around on the grass.

"Charlotte," said Hannah, "could you come here, please?" When Charlotte ran over, Hannah pulled a Kleenex out of her pocket and wiped Charlotte's nose. "Okay," she said, and Charlotte ran off again.

"How old are you now?" I asked Hannah. I hated the sound of it. I was making polite adult small talk with Hannah, in deference to her new, grown-up look, but what I really wanted to ask her was, "What are you wearing to school tomorrow? Who's your best friend? What's she like?"

"Thirteen," she said, which surprised me. I'd thought older.

"Seventh grade?" I asked.

She nodded.

"Do you like it?"

"Yeah," she said. "It's okay." I was really boring her, I could tell. She turned her face toward the ball game.

"I don't think I liked seventh grade much," I said. "I guess I thought thirteen was a hard age."

Hannah turned her face to look at me then, slowly. "I *know*," she said. I watched her eyes get big.

"You know my brother, right? He's in the tenth grade?"

She leaned toward me. "*He's* the one who's got all the good stuff. He's got a CD player, and a cassette deck, and a computer, and a phone in his room. And, he's allowed to do whatever he wants, but *I* have to do all the work around the house!"

"You do?" I said.

"Yes!" she said. "Because he's too *busy* to do his chores. And my sister?" She gestured at Charlotte. "Of course she's too little to help, but she gets *way* more toys than I do. It's not really fair. She gets all the attention."

Hannah leaned closer to me. "And my dad," she said, raising her eyebrows confidentially, "he thinks I get along with my stepmom *so* well, but I don't."

"This is the worst part, though," she said. I had no idea what she was about to tell me—I was trying to remember what, at that age, could be so bad.

"I used to have these imaginary friends?"

"Friends?" I said, stupidly.

"There were four or five of them."

I waited, but she didn't say anything else.

"What were they like?" I asked Hannah. "Your friends."

"Oh," she said, slowly. Seeing them. "They were . . . I don't know. It was a long time ago."

"Well, what happened to them?" I asked.

"My brother killed them," she said matter-of-factly; she let my shock wash by. "We were in the car one day, and my brother was being really mean to me. He threw them out the window."

"Oh, no," I said.

"But I revived them!" she said. Her face had become animated again. Her eyes were wide and glistening. "I pulled them back in. Then he squashed them." She made a mashing motion with her two palms. "But I said, 'They're flexible!' and I stretched them back.

"Then he gave them poison," she said, "but I had the cure."

The brother did a few more things to them, I can't remember them all. Then she said, "Finally I just left them dead."

"*Why?*" I said, and I watched her come out of herself, look at me as if I was, after all, just another inscrutable grown-up.

She shrugged. "I don't know," she said. "That was the last time I saw them. On that car ride."

When she looked back at me, something had changed. I could see it, Sarah—her leaving one place in her memory and entering another. She sighed.

"I really loved them a lot," she said, with nostalgia. "There was this one—I remember—he was a dog with one blue eye and one brown eye, and a floppy ear."

That's all I wanted to tell you, Sarah. The thing that seemed so important, that day. I remember a time when a thought wasn't fully a thought until I had told it to you—you and your mom would drop me off and I'd go to my room and visualize you in the car, count the blocks and the minutes until you walked in the door and up to your room and I could talk to you again.

"What happened to Sarah?" Katrin said to me on our walk that day.

"Nothing happened to Sarah," I said. "We just grew up. We're grown-ups now."

"Tell me a story about her," Katrin said.

"Oh, Katrin," I replied.

You were the only one who knew I was pregnant, those last few weeks in San Francisco. That last night, just before I left to go home to Massachusetts for good—we had finally found some time to give each other, when it was too late—you drove gamely all the way across town to get me, because the smell of the bus nauseated me too much by then. We decided to make supper at home instead of going out, so we went to the grocery store and walked down all the aisles twice. Finally we found something that looked okay to me—plain eggs.

"Take your eggs," you said to me, at the end of the night. I laughed when you tried to hand me the carton as we were going out the door.

The other thing I left in your house was the unused half of the home pregnancy test two-pack I'd bought, unable to resist a bargain. Packing up my apartment to leave, I'd stood paralyzed in the bathroom, holding the leftover tester. Either way—keeping it, throwing it out—seemed like bad luck, or tempting fate, so I put it back in the medicine cabinet and grabbed it just as I was leaving to see you that last night. At your apartment, I pulled the box out of my jacket pocket on my way to the bathroom and asked, "Do you think you might ever need this? Should I leave it?"

"I hope not," you said, and, "Sure." I set the box under the bathroom sink, next to a huge box of condoms you'd bought and never opened, and we made a few dispirited jokes about the juxtaposition, and the recent departure of Rick, the papaya-enzyme-munching publicist who had left you just when you thought things were going really well, to "sort things out in L.A.", which, of course, meant sleep with his ex-girlfriend.

I remember I knew it as soon as I met him. Even before he started in on the benefits of papaya, did an alarming pantomime at the dinner table of an enzyme with beaver teeth, munching away in his own gut, I thought, this man isn't so great, and I got a picture of us in junior high, Sarah—it made me smile in spite of the circumstances— with our tortured hair, our kettle-cloth shirts; and I had the sudden thought that nothing much had changed since then, since Brad Barrows stuck a nail in your arm in Life Science because you turned around to look at him one too many times; and Dirk Jensen abandoned me at the Girls' Day Dance and I walked, crying, two miles to your house in my Qiana halter dress and blue wedgies, to wait for you.

"Tell me about your room," Katrin said.

My room was on the third floor, and the big sycamore tree in the side yard scraped against my window. The purple and green and turquoise wallpaper I'd picked out made the room look dark and cool. But it was never cool, remember? When you stayed over, we'd lie on my bed on our backs, side by side, in T-shirts and underwear, no covers, a fan in the window blowing hot air over our bodies.

"Your purple and blue dresser," Katrin prompted. "Your mirror with the lightbulbs around it. Tell me about those hot roll things you and Sarah used to put in your hair to make it curly."

"Do you still have the raft, Mom?" Katrin asked me once.

"Oh, no," I told her. "Maybe Sarah does."

I remember the last time we used it, though, driving back from a hot, aimless trip to Wyoming. I was leaving for college in a week. We'd been paralleling a bright, flat river lying on the other side of a barbed-wire fence for miles, when suddenly you pulled over and turned off the ignition, got out of the car and walked to the trunk without saying anything.

"What are you doing?" I asked, following you.

"Let's run the rapids," you said.

"Here?" There were no rapids. The river, beyond the fence, took a turn and went under the highway, came out on the other side into more of the same, flat landscape and continued away. While I was trying, futilely, to see what was under the bridge, you hauled the raft out by yourself, carried it to the fence and heaved it over.

"*Sarah!*" I said. You just looked at me.

"Are you coming?"

Where this distance between us had come from, I had no idea, but, I knew, we weren't ourselves that day. The whole drive I'd been wishing we hadn't come, that we were back in one or the other of our rooms, lying on our stomachs on the bed, or sitting on the floor, working on some project: our monthly Boy Rating Charts, or finger-nail repair, or earring inventory, or anything.

You shrugged, then you turned and climbed through the fence, dragged the boat to the river, shoved off and got in. With perfect concentration, you dipped the paddle in the water, looking straight ahead, your eyes focused on what was coming up, that I couldn't see.

I ran to the other side of the road and waited. It seemed like it took a long time, but it probably didn't. Just when I began to get frightened, the raft emerged. You were no longer paddling—you were sitting, straight-backed, with the paddle in your lap, and I remember that you looked still and changed, floating from the dark shadow of the bridge back out into the glaring light. The moment you came out of the tunnel, I was mad at myself for not having gone with you—as if, in that half-minute, I had given up something large.

The short trip seemed to have improved your mood, though; in the car, you were talking to me again. "What am I going to do without you, Abby?" you said.

That last night in San Francisco, three years ago, now, we talked until late, sprawled on your bed in front of the television, then you drove me home. You got out of the car, walked me to the door of my building, and gave me a hug. "I'm going to miss you," you said, and I've thought about it since. In that moment I almost asked you, "Who?" Who were you going to miss? I can't remember why I had the momentary thought, as I stood there feeling lost and empty-handed in my changing body, the small, secret life inside me taking root pointlessly, that if I knew who you meant—who it was you saw, when you hugged me good-bye—it might help me feel less alone.

You probably still have those eggs, unless you've moved again. For a while after I got back to Massachusetts, I made a joke of calling every couple weeks, to see if you'd thrown them out. "It's me," I'd say into your machine, and, "call me," until suddenly, one day—like when you're a kid and you repeat something over and over until it loses its meaning—the words sounded odd and frightening, coming out of my mouth. The last I heard from you was a Christmas card: HAPPY HOLIDAYS, LOVE, SARAH, it said inside, and

I'd stood in the kitchen holding that piece of paper for a long time—until all the light had left the room and I couldn't see the four words anymore—before I threw it in the garbage.

Here's one last thing I want to tell you, Sarah—a parting gift, maybe. I can't do this forever, I don't think. One day I asked Katrin why she was pressing her fists into her closed eyes. "I'm trying to see something," she said. When I asked her what, she said, "You know how sometimes you can see pictures of things on the insides of your eyes?"

"Mm-hmm," I replied.

"Well, once I saw a wavy bright red tablecloth with little pictures of golden apples with golden leaves on golden branches, and little golden wheelbarrows."

"Really?" I said. "That must have been beautiful."

"It was," she answered, fists to her eyes.

She has faith she's going to see it again.